The Aztec Chronicles

The Aztec Chronicles

The True History of Christopher Columbus as narrated by Quilaztli of Texcoco

a novella

by

Joseph P. Sánchez

TQS PUBLICATIONS

A Division of Tonatiuh-Quinto Sol International, Inc.

Post Office Box 9275 Berkeley, California 94709

First Printing: May 1995

Library of Congress Cataloging-in-Publication Data

Sánchez, Joseph P.
The Aztec chronicles : the true history of Christopher Columbus, as narrated by Quilaztli of Texcoco : a novella / by Joseph P. Sánchez
p. cm.
ISBN 0-89229-030-7
1. America--Discovery and exploration--Spanish--Fiction. 2. Indians of North America--Mexico--Fiction. 3. Columbus, Christopher--Fiction. 4. Explorers--America--Fiction. 5. Explorers--Spain--Fiction. 6. Aztecs--Fiction. I. Title
PS3569.A46764A97 1995
813'. 54--dc20 95-4312
CIP

ISBN: 0-89229-030-7

Dedication

Dedicated to the struggle
of all indigenous peoples
against colonial forms

Acknowledgement:
A special note of thanks to my wife,
Clara Castillo Sánchez,
for her inspiration and literary criticism
in the writing of this novella.

The Chronicles

tenochtitlan

The Major Characters

Quilaztli
Aztec historian and narrator of the Aztec Chronicles

Copil, Tlacaellel, and Yoanizi
Aztec high priests of the
Cult of Huitzilopochtli

Tilini, Tleume, and Caudi
The three spirits who preside over the
tribunal in the case against Cristóbal Colón

Cristóbal Colón
Christopher Columbus, Admiral of the Ocean Sea,
who signed his name Cristo Ferens (Christ-bearer)

Diego Colón
Legitimate son of Cristóbal Colón

Fernando Colón
Illegitimate son of Cristóbal Colón

Martín Alonso Pinzón
Captain of *Pinta* in the voyage of discovery

Alonso Sánchez
Unknown Mariner who discovered America in 1484

Bartolomé de Las Casas
Friend of the Colón family and editor of
Colón's journals

Hernán Pérez Mateo
Loyal follower of Martín Pinzón

Rodrigo de Triana
First to sight land in the wee hours of 12 October, 1492

Peralonso Nino
Pilot Major of *Santa María* under Colón's command

Cristóbal García
Of *Santa María* who helped fake Colón's logs

Juan de Coloma
Personal clerk and notary of King Ferdinand and
Queen Isabel

Isabel
Queen Isabel

INTROIT

I was born Quilaztli, fifth son of Tizoc the Elder.

I was born in the year Ce-Acatl, or, by your calendar, in the year 1467.

I am the keeper of my people's past, our present, and our future.

I am not a prophet, such things are left to the priests who belong to the cults of Huitzilopochtli and Tezcatlipoca.

I am an annalist, an historian, if you wish. I am he who writes and interprets the meaning of the continuity of our world view.

The great emperor Moctezuma II would come to me for advice, as did his prophets.

Once, he came to ask about rumors that were troubling him, rumors regarding his death and that of his people. He was last here in the Christian year 1518 when his spies reported that they had seen white bearded men on our eastern coastline.

It is true that he feared the return of the Tolteca god Quetzalcoatl who is represented as a feathered serpent. In our world view, he was exiled by the Cult of Tezcatlipoca for more than 500 years but he threatened to return from the east and retake what rightfully was his.

When the bearded white men landed on our shores, Moctezuma believed, as did others, that Quetzalcoatl had returned.

It was in that year that the gods Tilini, Tleume and Caudi gave me the power to see 500 years into the future. My burden is to keep alive the history of my people. That is my lot....

My history could fill many houses. To write it, I passed through light and darkness. I was willing to die to learn of the unknowable.

I present what I know to you.

I write my story as I learned it, in an out-of-body experience, for I was rendered unconscious by the Azteca high priests of the Cult of Huitzilopochtli: among them Tlacaellel, Yoanizi, Copil, and others who did not survive the ordeal.

It was they who put me in contact with the spirits, Tilini, Tleume and Caudi. Although I wrote the history you are about to read, all of the words and images in it are nothing more than the spirit world's views of man's inhumanity to man.

It was at a secret shrine outside of Tenochtitlan, high in the mountain range known today as Mil Cumbres. There, the high priests summoned the gods. Tlacaellel and his colleagues knew that I had become obsessed with the idea of "seeing." To do this, I was willing to use their hallucinogens even though this was a very difficult decision to make.

"I want to see the truth," I declared to them as my heart nearly pounded out of my chest with fear.

"Are you prepared to lose your life?" asked Copil.

"All you will see is a glimpse of a fleeting world. It is a world that moves and changes, one with movements which you may never understand," added Yoanizi in a tone that sounded angry.

"I must do it," I managed to mutter. "I must. Even if it means my life, I. . . I must at least try!"

"Everything is dangerous," said Tlacaellel, a fatherly tone in his voice. "Life is one risk after another for those who dare — for those who seek knowledge beyond that of their time. All of us here will journey into the unknown with you, even though we know that we, too, may perish."

"We have not attempted to contact Tilini, Tleume and Caudi for 23 years," said Copil. His voice trembled at the mere mention of the three spirits. "What makes us so sure our mixtures will work? We must use the same potions that were consecrated the last time we tried. The herbs are old, the powders are old, the oils are old, and the urns are dried and cracked. It is too dangerous."

Tlaecallel, his head bowed, spoke with an air of finality, "The die is cast," he declared. "There is no turning back. We began our journey in this direction when we became priests. And we re-dedicated ourselves to it when we began our fasting after the last full moon. The incense that burns in the temple of Tenochtitlan has signalled the beginning of what we must complete this night. The herbs, the powders, the oils, the sea-foam, the wolf's blood, the blood and excrement of the frog-like creature, the acuecue-yxoyalotl, and the other potions from the temple cannot be returned from this mountain shrine, except by Tilini, Tleume and Caudi. If anyone here fears to take the next step, let him renounce his priesthood now!"

No one moved. Stunned by Tlaecallel's words, the priests sat silent for a long time. I was soon shaken from my numbness by Copil who handed me a cup of a vision-inducing potion made from an herb called tonatiuh-yxiuh. At the time, I did not realize it had already gone around to everyone else. The potion was the first taken in this and other rituals to rid the mind of fear. Sacrificial victims were given tonatiuh-yxiuh hours before their ordeals.

For the next few hours, around the great fire in the middle of the shrine, we took one potion after another as Tlaecallel, Yoanizi and Copil led the other priests in chants. The fire blazed with different colors.

The priests sang in a language I did not understand. My mind was spinning. My words were incoherent. I kept thinking about the guards that flashed through my mind. I remember holding someone's hand as I muttered, "Guardian, guardian...."

Tlacaellel's face appeared before me as he was turning to point behind him. Copil, his face splattered with blood, his long hair matted with blood and excrement, was holding a beating heart in his hands.

"That is the guardian," yelled Tlacaellel, "it is our protector from the other world."

"W-what other world? I don't see another," I said, almost incoherent.

"It's neither the world of the dead nor the living," said Yoanizi as he laughed in a mocking manner. "It is just another world. You will have to see it for yourself."

I fell deeper into a consciousness that was very near death. The phantasmagoria of my passage from life to death created a surrealism I never thought possible. I saw my deceased wife, Huipilli, young as when I last saw her, running naked among the reeds and flowers of Lake Texcoco. Laughing and taunting, she teased and beckoned me to her. But every time I approached her, she disappeared only to appear at another place.

Suddenly, I was sucked through a vortex filled with gases, pulled through the atmosphere as if I were falling from the sky. Then I passed through a bright, bluish light. On the other side was another world. It was indescribable, for it had neither sky nor earth, only light.

My body was numb, but I could still move.

I could see the other world, but at the same time I could see Tlacaellel jolting me, and slapping my face. I felt dizzy, my eyes were closing against my will. My head seemed to be exploding and in my body I had no feeling.

Copil continued to yell at me to wake me. He knew very well that, if I fell asleep, I could die. I opened my frightened eyes as wide as I could, but still I kept lapsing into unconsciousness. The efforts of the high priests to keep me alive were heroic, for they, too, were going through the same ordeal at the same time.

"Concentrate on this spot," Tlacaellel whispered as he pointed upward.

All I could see was a firefly in the general area to where he had pointed. I followed its every move as if it were moving very slowly. At times it moved far from me. Then it would move so close I could see every detail of its tiny body.

All of a sudden, I felt as if I had stood up to follow it, still within the confines of the shrine. The sensation of walking about was puzzling, for my body was lying helplessly on the ground. Then, as the firefly darted away from me, I had another sensation. I felt that I was looking across an expanse of time and space. It was then that I caught another glimpse of Huipilli. This time she wore a transparent veil that gave her nakedness a quality of godliness, for the veil was made of light and air. It contained stars and moons glistening within it. Huipilli smiled, pointed to her right, and disappeared.

I never saw her again.

I spun around to where she had pointed. What I saw jolted me to the center of my being. Standing a short distance from me were three gigantic spirits, Tilini, Tleume and Caudi. Handing me a quill and parchment, items that I had never seen before, Tilini ordered me to write in a strange language of which I had no knowledge.

"Write the word 'Introit,'" he said. "It is the first word of your search for truth. In order to sustain your clarity of thought, write, in the third person, every detail of tonight's experience, for your search has already begun. You will be all-knowing of the affairs of man." Then, as if mustering his ancient powers, Tilini spoke in a low voice and said, "Thou mayest know the unknowable that we shall share with thee this night."

Tleume whispered, "Start with what has happened here in the forest, and tell of what will have happened around you this night."

Spinning me around three times, Caudi transferred me to a Spanish monastery sometime in the future. It was there that, as an old man, I wrote my history in the third person, as I had been instructed.

I dedicate this history to my people, for I convinced them that a new order was at hand, and we must know its source if we were to overcome the destruction of the natural order of the Indian world by an historical force over which we, at this moment, had no control. It is through learning of the unknowable that we one day will triumph. The darkness through which we must pass is the historical lie that has been thrust upon us.

Our only weapon is the light of truth.

Our downfall began 500 years ago.

It began with a lie.

Chapter 1

The Death Scene, May 20, 1506

In Valladolid, Spain, Cristóbal Colón, gasping for air, lay on his death bed.

Severely crippled by arthritis which now was attacking the bones of his upper chest, his life ebbed slowly. Around him, his legitimate son Diego, and his bastard son, Fernando, knelt at his bedside. Behind them stood his sea captain friends Diego Méndez and Bartolomé Fieschi along with a few faithful family servants.

Colón's younger brother, Diego, quietly entered the room and knelt to pray. Standing at the foot of the bed, a servant assisted the parish priest to administer the viaticum. In a quiet, soothing voice the priest said, "I absolve you from your sins, *in nomine patris et filii et spiritu sanctis.*" The word "amen" quietly made its way around the room, punctuating the centuries old ritual.

Rapidly weakening, Cristóbal Colón whispered almost inaudibly, *"In manus tuas, Domine, commendo spiritum meum* —Into your hands, Lord, I commend my soul."

Hearing this, the priest hastened the last rites. Quickly, he washed the feet of the Admiral of the Ocean Seas in the ancient tradition inspired by the example of Jesus Christ. Then he blessed the holy water and the holy oil, and he anointed the Discoverer's forehead and feet. The pungent scent of burnt incense filled the dark, candlelit room. It gave the occasion a feeling of sacredness as if all were taking place in a church.

All the while, Diego, holding his father's right hand, marveled at his face. It was gaunt, yet there was a serenity to it, one which Diego had not seen in all the years he had known his father. *Perhaps,* he thought, *my father is resigned to leaving this world for a better one.*

Suddenly, the Discoverer opened his eyes. There was a glint of wildness in them. His mouth opened, as if wishing to say something. The startled priest grabbed a crucifix and anxiously looked around the room as if he had felt something enter. The candles flickered, some went out, yet there was no breeze or moving air in the room. The priest moved the crucifix in the air in the sign of the cross while he clutched a rosary in his left hand. Stiffening his crippled body and trying to rise, the Discoverer pointed westward, then he collapsed. He was gone. Diego and Fernando bowed their heads and made the sign of the cross. The muffled sound of weeping women came from the hallway.

Thousands of miles to the west, on a thickly forested mountain located to the south of Tenochtitlan, Quilaztli, an aged annalist from Texcoco, keeper of the sacred histories of the Aztecs, fell to the ground. His eyes were almost bursting from convulsions while his mouth foamed and his limbs twisted beyond belief. The stench of vomit, blood, urine and fecal excretions from his fevered body was unbearable. It was almost midnight, and the large fire illuminated Quilaztli's contorted visage in strange ways, as it did those of the Azteca priests who had worked the spell. Shadows from the flickering light danced on their faces.

Moments earlier, in a self-induced trance, Quilaztli had hallucinated from potions that he and the six Azteca priests had taken during their two-week, ritualistic fast. The traumatic ritual, during which they had dared summon the spirits of the dead, had rendered them totally oblivious to all around them.

Three spirits, each emitting fire from their extremities, stood before Quilaztli. One was called Tilini, the second Tleume, and the third Caudi. Like a wizard of ancient times, Tilini appeared translucent in his feathered headdress and long green cape filled with crescent moons and glittering stars. He held a crooked sceptre of light in his right hand. On his shoulder sat an iridescent monkey, symbol of the baser forces of light and darkness. The legendary monkeys were fabulous beings that possessed a duality. One side could bring unexpected misfortune, the other side, a boon. He suited the unpredictable nature of a spirit. Of the three spirits, Tilini alone had the power to transport mortal men across space and time.

The other two spirits, Tleume and Caudi wore capes and headdresses, one yellow, the other magenta. Like Tilini, they, too, carried scepters. And, also like Tilini, they each had an eye that formed on the inside of their left hand.

Neither of them had a symbolic mascot, like the monkey, but curiously, their translucent capes were filled with symbolism represented by swastikas, concentric circles and triangles as well as mandalas with expanding centers, all interplaying with crescent moons, stars and comets.

Tilini, now hovering over Quilaztli, blew into his unconscious body which had continued to twitch spasmodically. Suddenly, Quilaztli, brought back from death's threshold, sat up stiffly. As if in a deep trance, he began to speak in a strange tongue. Dazed from the ordeal, the drugged Azteca priests of the Huitzilopochtli cult, their hair matted with the vomit and blood of the hemorrhaging Quilaztli, struggled to understand his words.

Short-limbed and dark-skinned, Quilaztli's face resembled that of the large stone Olmec heads which were known to him and his people who lived along the eastern coast of Tabasco, Campeche and Yucatán.

The impish-looking Quilaztli from Texcoco, with almond-shaped, yellow-colored eyes, a flat nose and large lips, was once called an *hechicero,* or warlock, by the Spaniards.

He had seen the tall ship commanded by the Discoverer. He had heard of the large settlement of the Discoverer's people on a faraway island, and he had seen the men from the tall ship snatch young boys and girls from the Mayan coast north of the narrow stretch of land that connected the empires of the Incas and the Aztecas. And word had spread about another incident which had occurred in 1493, on the Christian calendar, about the men of the tall ships who had attacked a band of warriors on one of the "thousand virgin islands" which the Discoverer had named Santa Cruz. Quilaztli had heard these stories and others.

Once, he witnessed one of their landings when he was with a trade caravan north of the narrow stretch of land the Jicaque called Maya. It was June of the Christian year 1494, along the Honduras coastline. Quilatztli remembered that summer. It was while at the Jicaque village that the people stopped what they were doing and ran to an overgrown tree line on the edge of the beach. They ran to see the tall ships stopped in the water. The Discoverer and several others came to the shore on a small vessel as the people watched fearfully from the jungle's edge. From there they witnessed the Discoverer's people as they stuck a pole in the ground. Attached to the pole was a strangely colored cloth which waved in the wind. Then they heard him speak some strange words, and later, a thunderous sound frightened them as the air was filled with a strong-smelling smoke. Quilaztli would later learn that, on that occasion, the Discoverer had named the place, *Río de la Posesión* — River Where Possession Was Taken.

Still fearful, but curious, some of the people at the jungle's edge went out to meet the strangers. They went carrying trade items, roasted fish, red and white beans, and fowl. Quilaztli went among them.

One of the Spaniards, noticing Quilaztli's long hair that reached to his ankles, his unusual features and penetrating eyes, recoiled at his presence. Half amused, but nervous, the Spaniard said, "This man is an hechicero! Beware the warlock." At this, one of the more audacious of the Discoverer's men laughingly called him over, saying, "Hechicero, can you tell me what the future holds for your people?" Another, taking heart from the actions of the first, with a sneer of contempt, yelled, "Can you show us how to make gold from these wretched stones that fill your land?" Quilaztli would remember this moment, and, while he did not understand what the strangers had said, he would remember the sounds.

Hechicero, Quilaztli mouthed the sound of the word. *What could it mean? Why did the Discoverer's men single me out? What was their intent? Who was this man they called the Discoverer?*

These and other questions plagued the brain of Quilaztli. *Was the Discoverer a god? Was he a messenger of Quetzalcoatl, the great white Toltec god who swore to return from the east?* As he asked himself these questions, his eyes widened with disbelief.

Quilaztli's curiosity was piqued by the presence of the Discoverer. He noticed the man had fair skin, red hair and greenish eyes, and, unlike himself, a long, pointed nose. He wore clothing made of heavy cloth. His footwear, colored brown, was clearly from some sort of animal skin, but Quilaztli did not know how the footwear was made.

The fair-skinned man wore a great cape that looked almost black. Quilaztli thought it was a dark blue dye that had been used on it. Under the cape, the Discoverer wore a white garment which covered his upper body. It was neatly tucked into a piece of brown clothing that covered his body from his waist to his knees. More clothing, white in color, covered his legs from the knees to his feet. Crowning his red hair was a peculiar-looking headdress made of the same cloth as the cape.

The voice of this man was different from that of the others who had arrived with him. It was quiet. Unlike the others, who dressed similarly, he seemed not to carry any weapons. Had he come in peace? In awe, Quilaztli thought that the man looked god-like.

The Discoverer's men began to hand the *indios* (a term the Spaniards used for the natives because they thought they were near India) some shell necklaces and shiny jingle bells which, ultimately, became the bane of the native world. While this was taking place, a foul-smelling Aztec priest from the Cult of Tezcatlipoca approached Quilaztli. As the priest rubbed an oily substance on Quilaztli's hand, he pointed to the Discoverer and whispered a prayer into his ear.

As the Spanish soldiers continued to make their way among the *indios,* Quilaztli approached the Discoverer. When no one was looking, he touched the strangely dressed man's clothing with the saturating sacred oil. It was believed that this act would make their lives one. Through the powers of the unctuous substance, the Aztec historian thought he would now be able to learn more of the Discoverer and whence he came. Now that he was standing next to him, Quilaztli noticed one more detail. The man was tall. "He was about two hands taller than I," he would say later.

Weeks passed after this event, and Quilaztli, now back in Texcoco, was summoned to the Aztec capital of Tenochtitlan. There, he prostrated himself before Moctezuma the Elder and told him all that he had seen and learned about the Discoverer. After he had spoken, the Aztec court sat motionless and quiet for a long time. The question, *What did it all mean?* nagged them, for they had no answer.

Not until years later, when he lay at the door of death on the thickly forested mountain top south of the Aztec capital, did Quilaztli learn the answer. Although he would survive the wrath of the guardian spirits, Tilini, Tleume and Caudi, for having summoned them, he would keep their secrets as long as he could.

Only he would know that the Fifth Sun was at its end.

Tilini had given him a mission: to write the history of the past, present and future of the encounter between the Discoverer's people and Indian America.

Fourteen years would pass before Moctezuma the Younger would journey to Texcoco to beg Quilaztli for the answer to the riddle of Quetzalcoatl.

By then, Quilaztli had amassed an archive filled with scores of Mexican histories from pre-European times to a time 500 years into the future. But despite his tremendous knowledge, the three spirits had instructed him never to use his knowledge of the unknowable in order to intervene in human affairs. Because of that, Quilaztli was powerless to stop what would happen next.

Meanwhile, on May 20, 1506, time stood still.

Both men lay dying; one in the comfort of a European bed, and the other on the earthen floor of a forested shrine.

The death of one meant the death of the other. Although Quilaztli would actually die years after the Discoverer, he would live long enough to see his people as a dying race. Quilaztli's death, which began at that instant, would be slow and filled with anguish.

As Cristóbal Colón lay dying in Valladolid, Tilini, Tleume and Caudi appeared at his deathbed and filled him with regret. He saw the future. As his last gesture he pointed west, toward the setting sun, the dying sun of the Aztecs and Indian America. The same perishing sun also foretold the destruction of the Columbian dream.

At the very moment of Colón's death, Tilini, Tleume and Caudi snatched his soul and took him to stand judgement in the forest before Tlacaellel, Yoanizi and Copil, the drugged high priests who had appointed themselves an Aztec tribunal. Colón would also stand before Quilaztli.

Their revenge would be a lasting curse on the descendants of Cristóbal Colón. They would show him how his discovery for Spain, and his ill-begotten treasures, would come to naught.

The guardians of eternity, Tilini, Tleume and Caudi, knew it would all be done precisely in the way of all eternity, in the flash of an eye blink.

Chapter 2

Dies Irae

The wind blew cold air over the forest as the full moon brightened the spaces between the fast-moving clouds. Tlacaellel and the other priests tried to keep the fire going despite the strong gusts of howling wind that appeared to pound against it. Quilaztli continued to speak in a strange tongue.

Tlacaellel talked the others into beginning the ritual again so they could join Quilaztli in his quest for eternal justice. The next few hours were crucial.

The hallucinogenic potions were doubled as the Aztec priests began to convulse and cleanse their bodies of impurities through excretions, as Quilaztli had done. Two of the priests died in the process. Another, unable to make the transformation, fell into a deep coma, never again to regain consciousness. Leaving their bodies, the high priests Tlacaellel, Yoanizi and Copil crossed the wasteland between life and death. Momentarily suspended in time and space, they joined Quilaztli at the instant of Cristóbal Colón's death.

The three Aztec priests sat like judges on a tribunal. They felt all-powerful, for now they could understand the strange tongue of Quilaztli. It was the same as that spoken by the Discoverer and his people. The spirits Tilini, Tleume and Caudi, surrounded the soul of the Discoverer, thus obstructing the soul's passage to his creator. Now, Colón, as he listened to the tribunal speaking in Spanish, could understand their threatening questions.

"¿Sabe porqué lo hemos llamado?" asked Quilaztli, the Aztec historian. His mind's eye pierced through the Discoverer's soul.

"¡No!" answered Colón. He did not know why he had been summoned.

"¿Sabe porqué no permitimos que su espíritu pase a su propio destino?" queried Tlacaellel. He, too, glared at the soul of the Discoverer.

Colón answered, "¡No!" He had never expected that his soul could be detained other than in Purgatory, in accordance with Christian doctrine.

"¿Sabe porqué tenemos que hacer este proceso contra los hechos de Cristóbal Colón?" shrieked Copil. His patience with the prisoner had grown short.

"¡No!" whispered Colón, perplexed.

"Entonces no sabe porqué está aquí," laughed Yoanizi. He jeered at the defendant who, soon, would be allowed to speak for himself in this, his first moment of eternity.

Colón looked about him. The nebulous, ethereal setting was nothing more than the warm, bright light he had seen an instant before his death in Valladolid. No, he could not comprehend why he was there. He knew that at the moment of his death he saw the spirits Tilini, Tleume and Caudi standing there, among the living around his deathbed. He remembered that he was drawn through a tunnel by an invisible force, and, seeing a magnificently bright blue light at the end of it, he recalled being enveloped by its warmth. Suddenly, a hand reached out to him. In his excitement he grabbed it. At that instant, he felt a tinge of dread. It was Tilini's hand, and the spirit would not turn it loose.

"Before we let you see the future of your discovery," said Quilaztli in a heavy Nahuatl accent, "tell us, in your own words, how you began this quest that led you to cross the ocean?"

The Aztec priests thought they already knew the answer, but the life of Cristóbal Colón held secrets which would need to be purged if the tribunal's judgement were to be just. The spirits Tilini, Tleume and Caudi made certain to control how much of the future their Aztec mortals could see. If Quilaztli were to write the history of the future impact of Columbus's actions, he would need to know its past. As Colón began to speak, Tleume and Caudi departed suddenly.

"Sometime around 1480," whispered Colón, "after I had learned how far the Portuguese had sailed southward, I began to think that if they could sail south to the equator and return, despite their small ships and scant supplies, why not try sailing west to get east—to India, or China, or the Spice Islands of the Antipods.

I knew the Portuguese were stuck at the equator because they had lost sight of the North Star and were afraid to proceed any further without its guidance. Once they got to within 8 degrees of the equator, they lost confidence to navigate further south. I reasoned that by sailing west, and by keeping my ship north of the equator, I would always be in full view of the star. And, I figured if the Portuguese caravels held enough food and water for three months, my ships could do the same. I could sail west for three months, and strike the Japanese island of Cipangu before my supplies ran out. That was my plan."

Chapter 3

Ecce Homo

Quilaztli, the historian, and Copil, Tlacaellel and Yoanizi, the high priests, sat motionless. Colón had summarized his position as expected. Yoanizi, slowly speaking in Spanish so he could be understood, began the next series of questions.

"Tell us where you...."

"Tell them about your plan, you thief," a thunderous but familiar voice rang out in the forest, interrupting Yoanizi.

Colón's spirit looked about in dread, for the voice was that of Martín Pinzón. He had been summoned from eternity by Tleume and Caudi.

"The man they call the Discoverer is a fraud. I, Martín Alonso Pinzón, commander of the *Santa María,* native of Palos and witness to the fraud perpetrated on the world by this so-called Discoverer, know the true story of a life based on a lie. I am here to testify to the truth for all eternity to know."

"Tell us," said Yoanizi, the Aztec priest, "so we may better judge the character of this man, the Discoverer, and thereby know by what standards our future has been predicated. Tell us, so we may learn why the gods have foresaken the Indian world, and why they have delivered us into the hands of a fate which began with a lie."

"The man called 'the Discoverer,'" explained the spirit of Martín Pinzón, "was a man without a country. Some say he is a Jew, others claim he is Catalán or Aragonese. Still others keep repeating that he came from an unimportant principate called Genoa. Yet, he spoke Italian badly, if at all. Why, he didn't even write it!

In life he spoke Portuguese and Spanish, and he was quite literate in both languages. He said he was Genoese. He even claimed to be a trader on the Mediterranean, but word had it he was nothing more than a pirate, preying on Spanish shipping. Tell them, Colón, in front of me, as God is your witness. Who are you?

Tell them how you dreamed up your plan to make yourself the richest man on earth, and tell them how you lied about the discovery after you had learned that I had died one week after returning to Spain.

My death opened the door for more of your lies and the suppression of the truth. Tell them that you are a native of Pontevedra in Galicia, Spain. Tell all that, so there will be no difficulty in conceding the possibility that you are not the true discoverer.

Admit that your father was Domingo de Colón, known by the soubriquet of *'El Mozo* — the boy,' and that your mother's name was Susana Fonterosa. Tell them, Colón, so they may learn of a fate that began with your lies."

"Tell us!" demanded the haunting voices of the Aztec tribunal.

Colón spoke, in a raspy forlorn tone, barely audible above the gusts of wind in the forest. "I know only that my deed has led to the discovery of a route from the confluence of the Río Tinto and the Río Odiel near Palos and the Spanish monastery at La Rábida to the Canary Islands, thence to the continent now called America, and back to Spain. I alone am the mastermind of such a discovery. Pope Alexander VI confirms this, and history will record it. There are no true witnesses to the contrary."

Suddenly, a bolt of lightning struck in their midst, setting fire to a tree which illuminated their arboreal surroundings. The winds stopped, and before them Tilini, spirit guardian of eternity, stood with a bundle of papers in hand.

Quilaztli took the bundle and read quickly through the papers. Raising his eyes, he spoke.

"These papers are signed by the Royal Fiscal Villalobos, who states that the word of the discovery went from mouth to mouth in every port and town in Andalusia. But, according to those who heard it with their own ears, from the lips of Spanish mariners who sailed on the expedition, they learned of a different discoverer.

Villalobos says that the Vatican — the Pope — upon referring to the discovery for the first time in a Papal Bull, employed only ambiguous terms. The Pope avoided calling Colón the discoverer.

Aware of accusations against Colón, the Pope was therefore timorous of compromising the Papal Infallibility by naming Colón the discoverer."

Quilaztli, pausing for a moment as he scanned the papers before him, then looking around, said, "It matters little whether Villalobos alleges that it was Pinzón. The truth is that it was another, not Cristóbal Colón!"

Colón muttered, almost inaudibly, "It is as I have

said."

"Tell them the truth!" shrieked the voice of Alonso Sánchez. The sound of the voice shook Cristóbal to the core of his being. "I, Alonso Sánchez, pilot of Huelva, whose very name and authority he has never mentioned, whom he has deliberately concealed from his majesties... I, Alonso Sánchez, am the true discoverer!"

Held in the grip of the spirit, Tleume, the ghostly image of the ancient mariner broke loose and moved toward the tribunal of Copil, Tlacaellel and Yoanizi.

"I am the Pilot of Huelva," he said, "the master of a nao which I navigated for many years between the ports of Spain, the Canary Islands and the Madeiras in the Ocean Sea. I am the 'other' to whom you refer. My deeds will be sung one day by the soon to be famous historian and captain, Gonzalo Fernández de Oviedo y Valdez. He will pronounce the *vox populi* regarding my discovery of a route from Spain to the unknown continent and back. He will also deny that which has already been denied by the men of Palos and the Crown of Castile which has refused to accede to the unlimited claims of Colón in the fraudulent statements written in the opening remarks of the Capitulations of Granada, Colón's contract from the Catholic Majesties, supposedly giving him all rights *in perpetuo* to his discovery."

"Why do you stand before us with nothing to add to what is already known?" yelled Yoanizi, the Aztec priest, as he pointed a challenging finger at the ancient mariner.

"Leave us if you have nothing else to say," spoke Tlacaellel as if he were the chief inquisitor.

"Wait!" uttered Copil, the high priest. His voice was urgent. "I see a tall ship tossing in the sea. The tempest has driven it from the Canaries. Every one is struggling to turn the ship, but the hand of fate is pulling it out to sea. Further and further it is pulled until they pass the last known mark in the sea, filled with seaweed, a place known as the Mare Sargassum. Everyone on board is terrified beyond belief, including its captain — Alonso Sánchez. Suddenly, after many weeks at sea, they strike land. The mariners kiss the earth and lie there thanking their god for their deliverance from a most horrible death. The land is a large island unknown to them. The natives there give them food, water, fuel, and gold.

After they are strong again, the mariners leave on their tall ship and try to return to Spain along a warm current that carries them northeasterly. After endless struggles, they safely reach the Madeiras. But they have suffered many deaths. Alas, only Sánchez and four others have survived the ordeal!"

"I affirm all that has been said," spoke the voice of the ancient mariner, "and I add that the mysterious island upon which we landed is today called Santo Domingo. During the voyage I kept a chart of the route we had followed, going and coming, of that epic journey into the unknown waters of the Ocean Sea.

Being driven by the powerful easterly wind called the Levante, we reached the island after sixty days without surcease. My chart, made during that most trying time, was sufficiently correct so that anyone could make the same voyage again.

Oh, the knowledge we held in our grasp! It had eluded the Spanish, Portuguese, Andalusians, and the Basques who had looked beyond the shores of the Canaries, Madeiras and Azores for the last two centuries. They were sailors who had conscientiously followed the routes of the Phoenicians eighteen centuries before them!"

"How did you come to know Cristóbal Colón?" asked Tlacaellel.

"Upon our landfall on the Madeiras, at the island called Porto Santo in the Christian year of 1484," replied the moaning voice of Alonso Sánchez, "I heard that Colón lived there, working as a cartographer. My four companions and I went to him for assistance. Naturally, like musicians exchanging a new note to play, we compared what we knew of the known world.

He told us of his extraordinary dream to sail across the Ocean Sea. He showed us all of his papers, notes, charts, all this with a hurried voice, trying to impress us with his knowledge so that I, in turn, would divulge all I knew of the Ocean Sea beyond the Mare Sargassum.

I was ill, too ill. He knew it. Seeking a place to rest my weary body, I could not resist his generous, but self-serving offer of lodging in his home.

Totally worn out and feverish, I died in his house.

I know what this scoundrel did next! Colón, Clio's thief, told the people of Porto Santo that I had bequeathed all my notes, papers and charts for his library. He also said that I had given him my vessel in gratitude for the kindness that I and my wretched companions had received from him.

Unfortunately, no one existed who could defend our position. Since Portugal owned the Madeiras, the Portuguese chroniclers reported that they had knowledge that soon after my death, my four companions, the only survivors of my voyage to Santo Domingo, disappeared. No trace was ever found of them. The Portuguese, to this day, blame the Genoese for their mysterious disappearance. But all this was circumstantial. My companions were too ill to continue living.

What an auspicious time for the lucky Colón who now held our secrets and my chart. Yea, he sheltered us, and we died there."

Angry at the thought that he had inadvertently told Colón how to cross the Mare Sargassum, Sánchez continued.

"From us he learned of the route from the Canaries to Santo Domingo and back. And, with my papers in his possession, he went to Portugal, certain that he could make the discovery of the New World! I know with great certainty that from 1484 onward, he zealously, nay, fanatically, worked to convince the kings of Europe to finance his plan. . . nay, my plan!"

Quilaztli perceived the future of Colón's lie, and his face took on a pensive character. *The European historians would perpetuate it,* he thought. *They would record the "Columbian Legend." And each would write that after a long and lonely peregrination across Portugal and Spain, he finally reached the Court of Castile. There, no one would listen to him or take notice of his plan. His genius would be understood by no one, and he would be looked upon as a dreamer, as a visionary who worked for the betterment of mankind, or, at least, the non-Indian world.*

When finally someone listens to him, it is a Friar Antonio Marchena, a Franciscan, who happens to be the confessor to Queen Isabel. The good friar not only gives Colón and his son, Diego, food and lodging, he arranges for Colón to meet with Ferdinando and Isabel.

The lies go on and on, mused Quilaztli. *Did Isabel really sell her jewels to help finance the journey, as has been said?*

Was Colón an imposter? How could it happen that European historians would labor to perpetuate the myth that Colón was a genius, and also a martyr for whom Rome would solicit canonization? How could anyone consider him a saint, especially since he opened the door for the annihilation of millions of Indians at the hands of Europeans?

Still, on the face of it all, these were petty questions. But when measured against what would soon befall the Indian world, they nagged at Quilaztli's mind and soul.

How would he write his history of the future of this great encounter between two worlds—Indian America and Europe?

He reasoned he would describe the tragedy as an evil that began with a self-perpetuating lie.

"I need to know more about this lie before I can know what the future bodes for us," Quilaztli said to the spirits.

Chapter 4

Vincit Omnia Veritas

To learn more of the lie, the spirits Tilini, Tleume and Caudi allowed Quilaztli to drift ahead of the events in the forest.

Sixty years into the future, Quilaztli, accompanied by Tilini, found himself in the royal castle at Simancas, in Valladolid, a bucolic and rustic Spanish province north of Madrid. There he viewed a copy of a manuscript entitled *HISTORIA DE LAS INDIAS BY THE DOMINICAN FRIAR, BARTOLOME DE LAS CASAS.*

Las Casas was not only the Bishop of Chiapas, he was an intimate friend of Diego and Fernando Colón, the former the legitimate son, and the latter the bastard son of the Discoverer. Las Casas, who possessed many of Colón's papers, had been the only copyist of the journals written on the voyage of discovery.

Quilaztli discovered that one or more copies had been made before Colón had presented the original copy to Ferdinando and Isabel in Barcelona in 1492. He also discovered that the copies, in time, had disappeared. One copy had been in the possession of Las Casas, who made an abstract of it for his own use. He claimed he had quoted long passages from the original. But all that would exist, surmised Quilaztli, would be the Las Casas abstract.

How would his people ever learn the truth? To verify what had happened to the copies, Quilaztli moved five hundred years into the future and learned that all copies of Colón's journal had been destroyed. All that existed now was the abstract made by Las Casas. He found it in the Biblioteca Nacional de Madrid, a place where scholars from around the world came to study about the European colonial heritage begun by Cristóbal Colón. He also learned that Colón's bastard son, Fernando, had written a biography of his father entitled *HISTORIA DEL ALMIRANTE DON CRISTOBAL COLON*. He wrote it in order to discredit and deny the roles of Alonso Sánchez, Martín Alonso Pinzón and others in the discovery.

Like a detective, Quilaztli deduced that the idea was to protect the Colón family claim to the Americas by perpetuating the lie of the Columbian Legend. Almost all references to Alonso Sánchez had been obliterated by those now called the Colombinos—supporters of the Columbian Legend and claim to the New World.

All except one or two mentions, mused Quilaztli, for he knew that Gonzalo Fernández de Oviedo y Valdez had written of him in *HISTORIA GENERAL Y NATURAL DE LAS INDIAS* in 1535.

He also knew that the Inca, Garcilaso de la Vega, the Peruvian born mestizo historian had recorded in his *COMENTARIOS REALES DE LOS INCAS* that he knew of the incident of Alonso Sánchez of Huelva because he had heard it mentioned and described by some of the conquerers of Peru.

Strange, thought Quilaztli, *that these documents have been published and can be found in any library in the modern world, yet the truth has been so elusive. Why?*

Rapidly turning the pages of the Inca's *COMENTARIOS,* Quilaztli was eager to learn what the Indian side of Garcilaso de la Vega had chosen to tell of the truth he sought. The Inca's honesty almost jumped out of the pages. Quilaztli could not believe his eyes, but he was proud that the Inca was half Indian.

He turned to Chapter III and there, printed in bold letters, he read *HOW THE NEW WORLD WAS DISCOVERED.* The Inca had done his job. His words read:

"About the year 1484, one more or less, a Pilot,
native of Huelva, in the province of Niebla,
named Alonso Sánchez, sailed his small ship on
the Ocean Sea carrying merchandise from Spain
to the Canary Islands, which he sold there. From

the Canaries, he took fruit to the Island of La Madeira which he traded for sugar and other items that he took back to Spain. Working in this triangular trade, between Spain, the Canaries and La Madeira, he was hit by a tempest so swift and strong that he was unable to resist it. Pushed by the tempest, he ran 28 or 29 days without knowing where he was, for during that time he was unable to take a reference of the altitude either by the sun or by the North Star."

Fascinated, Quilaztli read on:

"...at the end of this long time, the wind died down, and they found themselves near a large island. It was not known which one, but it is suspected that it was the one now called Santo Domingo...it could be no other...because the Island of Santo Domingo is due west of the Canary Islands. Alonso Sánchez landed, and took a reading of the altitude of the unknown island. Later he described all that he had seen and all that had happened regarding his long voyage by sea from the Canaries to the large island to La Madeira. Lacking food and water and suffering from great fatigue caused by the sea voyage, the crew began to fall ill and die. Of the 18 men who had left Spain, only five reached

> La Madeira, among them the Pilot Alonso Sánchez of Huelva. They stopped at the house of the famous Cristóbal Colon, a Genoese, because they knew that he was a great pilot and cosmographer, and that he made navigation charts. Colon received them with much affection, and he gave them what they wished when he had learned what had befallen them in their arduous, drawn-out voyage, as they had told him. As they had arrived greatly fatigued, despite the aid Colón had given them, they were unable to recover, and they all died in his house."

Quilaztli sat quiet, almost stunned that the future world, if it let itself, could catch a glimpse of what he had learned in the forest north of Tenochtitlan. He knew that the Inca had written his words in 1560, and 500 years after Colón's discovery, Alonso Sánchez's discovery had not been completely obliterated. *But what did it mean?* he asked himself. *Will it take 500 years for the lie to die and Indian America to be set free from the evil of the European discovery?* Quilaztli's conundrum grew.

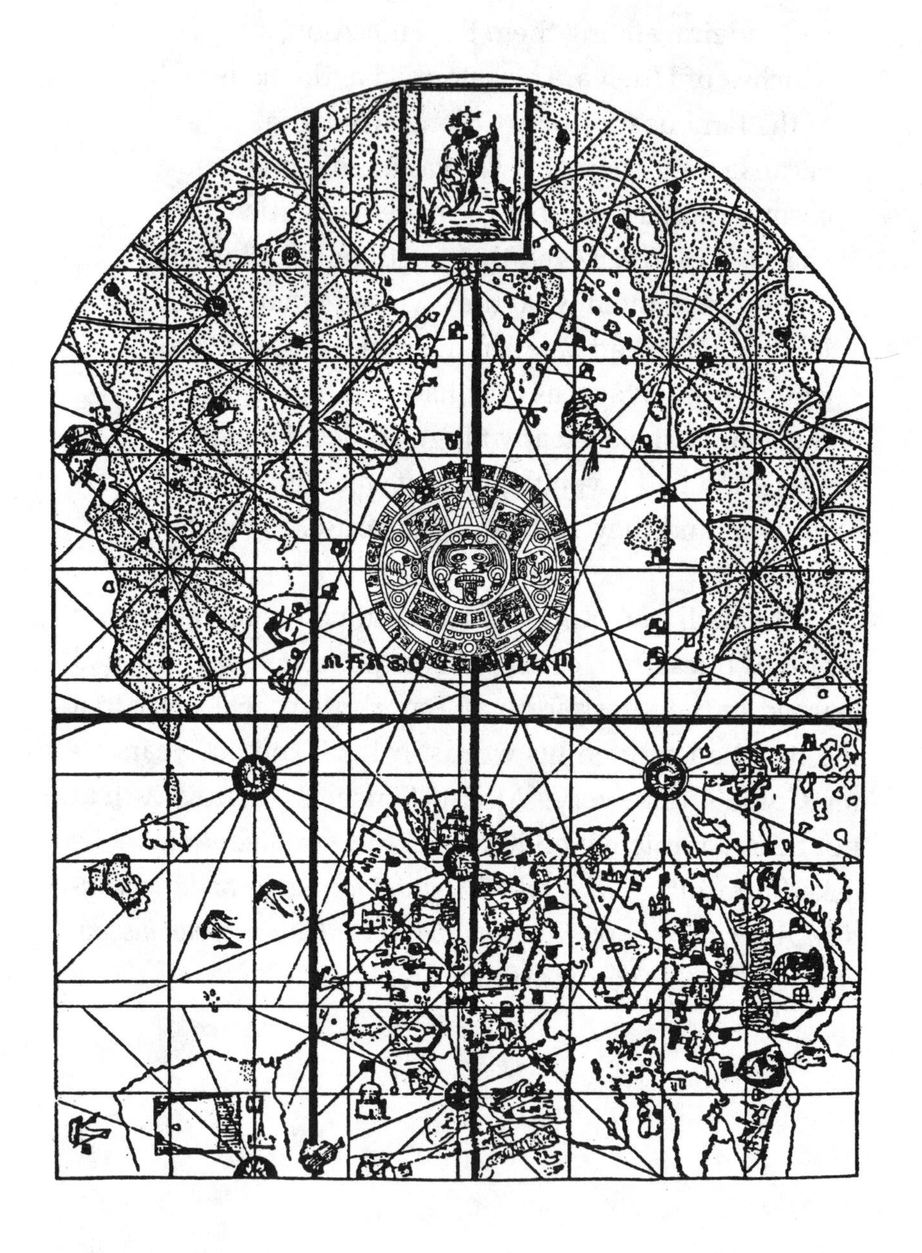

Chapter 5

The Canary Island Misconnection

The forest winds increased with renewed force, the clouds darkened, creating an opaque canopy so that the braziers of the Aztec tribunal produced the only light in the area. The priests, Copil, Tlacaellel and Yoanizi, pressed their inquisition against Colón. Each time he answered, "I am the true discoverer, your witnesses seek to destroy what I have done. History will absolve me."

"Tell us, Colón, about the maps of Alonso Sánchez," queried Copil.

"There were no maps left by Sánchez," responded Colón. After a moment, he said, "The only maps available to me were those drawn by the savants of the ancient world —Ptolemy, Eratosthenes of Cyrene, Hecataeus and others. They were, however, of little use to me. Mostly, they offered me consolation, for my studies of the unknown world were considered a joke by my Portuguese and Spanish peers. Hecataeus regarded the earth as a flat disk around which waters of the ocean flow. We knew that was not correct. I put my faith in the theory that the Earth was, indeed, round as Eratosthenes and other ancient savants had said. But Eratosthenes worked against me because his calculations of the circumference of the earth were too great. He estimated the earth to be nearly 25,000 miles in circumference. In order for me to convince Their Majesties of a shorter voyage, I had to tell them that the earth was only 11,000 miles in circumference — 18,000 at most. If the earth were presented as a smaller sphere, they would surely approve a voyage which would take only a small period of time. Furthermore, the crews would be more willing to risk a short voyage across the sea, away from land.

Although the Spanish court supported the figures of Eratosthenes as accurate, I was able to show that Hipparchus, the astronomer, had criticized the irregular work of Eratosthenes, and, in response to it, had proposed a parallel-meridian system of even intervals. On the maps that he proposed, he had divided the habitable world into eleven equally spaced intervals, the location of which he described in detail. For measurement of longitude, he proposed to make simultaneous observations of the moon's eclipses. This was an ingenious method, I must say, and I used it in my arguments against the supporters of Eratosthenes's calculations."

Cristóbal Colón paused for a moment in his long explanation about his knowledge of the world as it was described in his day.

"As for Claudius Ptolemy of Alexandria, I had read his famous eight volume *GEOGRAPHIA* to support my knowledge of the known world. In Volume VII, he lists 8,000 place names with latitudes and longitudes to determine their positions. Only a few of them were based on scientific observation, but his knowledge of them was taken from older maps and books which no longer exist. I wanted to convince Their Majesties that such places did actually exist, I could name them. If I were convincing enough, I could win their confidence. After all, Ptolemy's *GEOGRAPHIA* has one map of the world and 26 detailed maps all of which I had studied.

Ptolemy, too, supported my argument that the earth's size was smaller. All that was left for me was Posidonius's calculation. He said that one degree equals 500 stadia, a distance of nearly 58 English miles. The best my detractors could offer was that the earth was a circle and that a degree was merely one part of 360 degrees.

I never once disputed that a circle is not 360 degrees. But, I did maintain that one degree equalled 58 English miles at most, and if one multiplied 58 times 360, then the circumference of the earth could not be much more than

20,000 miles. Hence, I was safe in supposing that Posidonius would have supported my calculations. What better company than that!

It was from these interpretations that I concluded that Europe and Asia extended over one-half the circuit of the earth. Therefore, it was an easy matter to convince my supporters that I could reach Asia by sailing toward the west.

That is where I got my knowledge of the world— not from this Alonso Sánchez."

"Again, he lies!" interrupted Pinzón, "for we knew that Alonso Sánchez was blown off course for 30 days before reaching Santo Domingo. It is from Sánchez that Colón learned that the time and distance across the ocean could be closer than Eratosthenes had proclaimed. Except, and this is important, Colón overlooked one important factor — speed. The tempest had increased the speed of Sánchez's ship, thus cutting down the time to cross the Ocean Sea.

Colón had also argued that he had gained his knowledge from Paolo del Pozzo Toscanelli, the Florentine physician, whose hobby was to play with maps. He corresponded with Toscanelli for years. In order to draw attention from Sánchez's map, Colón invented the idea that Toscanelli had drawn a map showing the short distance from Spain to Asia—but he did not know about the route from the Canaries—that was accomplished by Alonso

Sánchez. It was Sánchez who pointed the way!

The existence of Toscanelli's chart was invented by Colón to defend against his having to declare publicly that he had learned of the route from the *piloto mayor*, Alonso Sánchez of Huelva.

Instead, Colón would have the entire world believe that his genius alone invented the route. In that manner, he could take full credit for the so-called discovery.

That is why his lie has been perpetrated and perpetuated, so that his family and future heirs, and no one else, can continue to profit from the exploitation of the Indies and its natives."

"Do you know this to be true? If so, how?" asked the Aztec high priest Yoanizi.

"I know this because I went to Italy myself and saw Toscanelli's map. I took copious notes from it and sketched it," responded Pinzón.

"What Toscanelli had drawn," he continued, "was nothing more than what was already known. The Florentine had noted Ireland and England in the north, the European continent showing Portugal and Spain, and the coast of Africa. The islands of the Azores, the Canaries and Cape Verde were also noted. The equator was his southern boundary. Across the Oceanus Occidentalis he showed Cipango, many small islands to the west of there and the coasts of Cathay, Quincai, Margi and Zaiton. The one remarkable aspect of his map was that all these places were set in a grid which made them easy to locate on a sea chart. The Portuguese were quick to pick up on the grid, for now they could sail south, past the equator, without worrying about getting lost. All they would do was sail from one grid pattern to the next. But, Toscanelli did not know that Alonso Sánchez had known about what lay in the Oceanus Occidentalis."

Angrily, Colón interrupted Pinzón, "That still does not prove a thing!"

To this, Pinzón retorted, "I trust that the forces of history and reason are sufficient to debunk the legend invented by the Colombinos. The truth shall be known," he pronounced. "It will be done here, this night in the forest." He said this with a knowing tone in his voice.

Then, raising his voice for all to hear, Colón spoke. "You," he began, "have not proven your case against me. Calling me a liar proves nothing. Your hypothesis of Sánchez's accidental discovery has been contrived to prove everything, but it proves nothing. God made me the discoverer so that I could bear Christianity across the Ocean Sea, as St. Christopher bore the Christ-child across the river. I, alone, have trusted in science to learn of all that can be known of this earth. And, as a scientist, I proved my hypothesis. You have proven nothing."

Collectively, the tribunal overseen by Copil, Tlacaellel and Yoanizi, whispered among each other that Colón also had not been honest about how he concluded that the Canary Islands would become his point of departure to the Americas. Why not the Azores? After all, they sit far out to the west in the Ocean Sea from Spain and Portugal. Colón had lived on the Azores, surely the people there, despite their Portuguese nationality, would have supplied him. After all, he had married a Portuguese woman. The tribunal was aware that Colón knew of the local stories that had flitted throughout the Azores for decades concerning another land far to the west. For years, strange looking cadavers had floated along the ocean currents and washed ashore on the Azores. Colón, himself, had studied their faces, their almond-shaped eyes, their clothing, or lack of it, and, on occasion, he had seen strange pieces of wood with markings on them. Strange plants and trees washed ashore as well.

Knowing all this, Copil asked again, "Why did he depart from the Canaries when he knew that west of the Azores he could strike land?"

"I was a master mariner," Colón spoke up. "I had been to sea from a very young age. I first went to sea in 1461, and, between the ages of 14 and 21, I had already been out several times. And, moreover, between 1482 and 1484, I had sailed down the African coast with the

Portuguese who had a trading post at São João da Mina, not far from the equator.

I already knew about the Canary Islands which one must pass before reaching the equator. I was familiar with the Ocean Sea from Africa to waters beyond England. Perhaps little note will ever be made of my voyage in 1477 to the Island of Tile, which some say is Thule, known on the *mappamundis* as Groenland. It is an island as big as England, but further north and west of there. When I was there the sea was not frozen, but the tides were almost 50 feet high and fell as much in depth.

The land lay, as I remember it, 73 degrees north latitude, not 63 degrees north as some have said. This I say to those who would doubt my knowledge of the sea and my lifelong interests in mysterious, yet undiscovered, lands. I had always lived in a seafaring community where everyone took an interest in what lay beyond the Azores, but Portugal, nay, England and France as well, were not disposed to support me.

I departed from the Canary Islands precisely because they were in Spanish hands, the very hands which supported the business venture I had proposed.

Furthermore, I say this to the tribunal: Pinzón did not tell you about all that was on Toscanelli's map — he left out mention of a strange island in the middle of the Oceanus Occidentalis due west of the Canary Islands.

I, Cristóbal Colón, have nothing else to say about the matter."

Chapter 6

Ultima Thule

Meanwhile, deep in the dark basement of the Archivo General de Simancas, the tall spirit, Tilini, who had transported Quilaztli to northern Spain, handed him a bundle of documents, one thousand pages thick, and, like a magician, turned to a page which read:

VENIENT ANNIS
SECULA SERIS, QUIBUS OCEANUS
VINCULA RERUM LAXET, ET INGENS
PATEAT TELUS, TIPHISQUE NOVOS
DETEGAT ORBES, NEC SIT TERRIS
ULTIMA THULE

These words, written by the great philosopher and

poet of Spain, Lucius Annaeus Seneca, author of Medea, who lived in Roman Cordoba during the first six decades after Christ, proclaimed to Quilaztli that the New World was known centuries before Colón's birth. Ancient mariners had frequented it from their half-way station on the Azores, the Hesperides of the ancient world. Colón, himself, had read the classical words of Seneca—

"AN AGE WILL COME AFTER MANY YEARS WHEN THE OCEAN WILL LOOSE THE CHAINS ON THINGS, AND A HUGE LAND WILL LIE REVEALED; TIPHIS WILL DISCLOSE NEW WORLDS AND THULE NO MORE WILL BE ULTIMATE."

Quilaztli could only marvel at Seneca's immortal words. *If,* he thought, *Colón had lived in the Azores with centuries old lore pointing west from there, why did he depart from the Canaries? Could the stories of Alonso Sánchez be true, thereby proving Colón a liar?*

"There are so many documents you must see," said Tilini, the spirit, "for your history must be able to describe them for the world to know. This archive holds an estimated 25 million pages of documents that describe what happened to your people in the first 328 years of European occupation. These musty, worm-eaten pages tell all that a mortal can know."

With a wave of his sceptre, Tilini declared, "Your mind will henceforth be filled with all that is stored here for you to use in the history which you must write for posterity. Now, let us leave here at once, for there are other records you must see."

With another wave of his crooked staff of light, the translucent Tilini ushered Quilaztli away from the Castle at Simancas to a great hall made of hewn stone. It had seven tables on one side, and three on the other. At each end of the dimly lighted hall were arched doors of glass, and behind each one hung a large, dusty purple curtain. On the side wall to the left of where Quilaztli was standing was another door which opened to a staircase leading downward and out to a large street.

On the opposite wall were three arched windows which overlooked a gloomy courtyard and three other halls, like the one where Quilaztli now stood. The halls completed a quadrangular shape.

Looking out of the windows to his right, Quilaztli caught a glimpse of a strange looking structure just as the moonlight passed through the clouds. Tilini whispered, "It is called the *Giralda* — a prayer tower used by the followers of Islam when they ruled the Spaniards. And this building was once called *La Casa Lonja,* the exchange house for merchants and the hated usurers, the money lenders who charged exorbitant rates of interest.

In 1758, the building was converted into the largest archive in the Spanish Empire. Over 44 million pages of colonial documents are stored here.

They, too, cover 328 years of colonial rule. All of these records tell the story of native peoples from Alaska to the Strait of Magellan, and from northern Africa to the Philippines.

They tell of the European thirst to control nature's treasures: salt, dyes, hardwoods and softwoods, plants and animals of all kinds, rivers, lakes, minerals — not merely content with gold and silver, they wanted to control tin, iron, copper and lead. The European exploitation of nature knows no bounds, and to accomplish their greedy end, they condemned your people and others to labor for them.

When Indian America could no longer do the work, the Europeans forced African slaves to do it. The documents contained here, in the *Archivo General de Indias,* tells that story.

Some of the documents here tell of Colón. Perhaps they can tell you something about a people whose fate began with a lie."

Quilaztli stood motionless in the hall that resembled the palatial tombs of Azteca emperors and princes. Like the usurers and merchants of the ancient *Casa Lonja,* royal counselors and their scribes came here to acquire and to exchange knowledge of the Americas. "This is the center of their knowledge about us," he concluded.

"Note," said the spirit Tilini, "this wealth of knowledge was stored in a place where the riches of the Americas were once counted and exchanged."

The irony had not escaped Quilatzli's notice.

"Here, and in Simancas," interrupted Tilini, "there were other centers, not the least of which were the great depositories in Mexico City, Havana and Lima. And I have yet to show you what the English, the Portuguese, the French and the Germans did to exploit Indian America. They, too, created large colonial archives. There is one final depository which you will see before this night is over. It is in a city called Washington, D.C. in the Americas. For now, I will direct you to the records of a legacy that began with a lie."

Over and over, Quilaztli studied the many documents in the wee hours of Sevilla's darkest night.

Chapter 7

The True Story of Colón's First Voyage

Threatening clouds gathered over the forest as the tribunal pressed its witnesses for more information. Tlacaellel's low, priestly voice resounded throughout the forest courtroom. "Tell us, Colón, — tell us about the voyage from the confluence of the ríos Tinto and Odiel. I want to know your version so that I may compare it with the other version that seems to be evolving here. We seek truth for posterity's sake, we seek wisdom that can be gained from such truth so that centuries from now, the Redman will know how the Whiteman dispossessed him of everything. Speak, Colón. Speak."

"Nothing I say here will change history," responded Colón. "I am not on trial here, for only my creator can judge me."

Hearing this, with the authority of a spirit guardian to eternity, an impatient Tleume shrieked, "If you do not respond to the high priest Tlacaellel, we will block your passage to the Creator forever. A soul without a resting place for eternity is condemned to oblivion. We can, and we will, disrupt the natural order of your spiritual life. Spiritual pain, Colón, is worse than physical pain. However, if you crave eternal anxiety and despair ...."

Colón reasserted himself forcefully. "I have nothing to hide and nothing to prove. My life speaks for itself. I am unmovable in what I have already stated. I change nothing. Precisely what is it that you wish me to explain?"

Hoarsely, Tlacaellel asked, "Tell us about the voyage."

Slowly, as if trying to comprehend the reason behind the question, Colón responded. "In life, I explained my claim to the New World in my suit against the crown. My depositions are in a large folder entitled *Escrituras* — writings."

"Did the crown believe your *Escrituras?*" queried Yoanizi.

"Most of it, yes, but my charge against the crown is another story that hinges on the same set of facts I will reveal here. I did receive permission from King Ferdinando and Queen Isabel to undertake the voyage in their name. My authority to command the expedition was based on the crown's statement that 'masters and crews of the naos should be officially constrained to go with the captain designate, they being paid the salaries and wages which reasonably and fairly should be due them for the period of the service they should be engaged in and perform.' As no one knew where we were going, I reiterated to the men the crown's words that they were to follow me to certain parts of the ocean on a very important matter in the service of God and Their Majesties.

It was no secret, however, that I had convinced Their Majesties of my plan to sail west to get to Japan and China. I met with resistance, nonetheless, for it was no light matter to recruit a crew to go in search of a land neither heard of nor known, much less under a commander, a stranger at that, who had shown up with a small child at the Monastery of La Rábida begging for bread, water and lodging.

No one believed in what I would ask them to do. Many laughed as if I were a fool or a visionary. They believed my project to be ill-planned and ill-fated. I, with the crown's order and God's guiding hand, determined to seize three vessels if that was what it would take to begin the voyage."

"How did you muster a crew for the expedition?" asked the priest, Copil.

"I had to resist employing force to the official measures," responded Colón, "although I did have authority to conscript crew members. Instead, I interpreted the crown's dictum to give me certain latitude in organizing my crew . . ."

"What did the crown authorize?" interrupted the priestly Tlacaellel.

"To do certain things in favor of our mutual interests, and to obtain the necessary crews for the three vessels," Colón responded, "I decided to use the only means left to acquire a crew. I turned to the town prisons and bargained with the criminals. In return for their services, I would obtain a Royal Order directing the suspension of criminal proceedings to any prisoner who would volunteer to follow me.

The order was given at Granada on April 30, 1492. The king explicitly stated, 'I DECLARE THAT IT IS NECESSARY TO GIVE SOME ASSURANCE OR SAFEGUARD TO THOSE WHO MIGHT ELECT TO GO WITH CRISTOBAL COLON, FOR IN ANY OTHER WAY THEY WOULD REFUSE TO GO ON THE SAID PROJECTED

VOYAGE; AND, ON HIS PART, IT IS BEING SUPPLICATED THAT WE SHOULD MAKE SUCH AN ORDER.' The point I make here is that not all crew members were friends or relations of the Pinzón Brothers. You have not queried those who did not have the same vested interests as the Pinzón faction which seeks to discredit me. Ask Diego Fernández Comenero and Feran Pérez Camacho, they see it differently."

"Again, I ask," responded an impatient Tlacaellel, "Tell us about the voyage, Colón. We are waiting to hear your version."

In a strong voice, the specter of Martín Pinzón spoke up before Colón could utter a word. "His version is in that fraudulent account that Las Casas concocted. Colón's life speaks for itself. If I may speak, I'll tell you what happened.

I was not surprised to learn that Colón had not the vaguest idea what he had gotten into. He was terrified once we departed the Island of Gomera, one of the Canary Islands. That was where we refitted the *Niña* and took on provisions and potable water. We heard that the Portuguese were out there somewhere trying to stop the voyage from taking place. It was rumored everywhere we went in the Canaries that the Portuguese planned to sabotage the voyage if they could find our ships. Once we got to the Sargasso Sea, I was summoned to the flag ship, the *Santa María.* I should say that the Sargasso Sea was as far out into the ocean as any human had ever gone —and Alonso Sánchez was the first to cross it. The Sargasso Sea was discovered by the Portuguese, led by the shipmaster, Pedro Velázquez de la Frontera, who had sailed for the famous Prince Henry the Navigator. We, the men of Palos and Huelva, knew about Velázquez's discovery from the many Portuguese sailors who stopped in our ports on their way to the Canary Islands and the Cape Verde Islands ...."

"Tell us about what happened when you boarded the flagship," snapped Tlacaellel with a sneer and a priestly tone of command.

"As I was about to say," replied Pinzón in a voice that said he knew well the ways of a commander, "I was given permission by Colón to board. The crew appeared anxious about my visit. At the time I was aware that there had been murmurings among them, critical of Colón. I knew that Colón wished to give up the quest. Indeed, some of the men were apprehensive of continuing the voyage — most of them were those aboard the *Santa María.* Once in Colón's quarters, he told me that the fleet must return to Spain. He was rambling, his voice was shaking, his eyes were wide. 'I propose,' he said, 'we return as soon as possible.' I was dismayed to hear such preposterous words. Angrily, I told Colón that the men follow me, not him. I reminded him that the ships were not his to do with as he wished.

I and the men of Palos were the real owners of the ships. Our investment in the expedition had been too great already. Calmly, I pointed out to him that there existed no real excuse he could give to Their Majesties for turning back the fleet.

In the first place, we had sufficient food and water to enable us to proceed, our men enjoyed good health, and their pride as trusted bearers of the crown's standards and the name of Spain would never permit us to return in disgrace, tarnished, as we would be, with the odious soot of failure.

I cannot help but repeat my response, which all aboard heard me yell at Colón — *Adelante, Adelante.* Forward, forward, even if it requires us a year to discover the land we seek, or perish in the attempt!"

"That is not true," responded Colón, his voice rising. "The men threatened to mutiny and Martín Pinzón was their mutinous leader."

In contrast, Pinzón lowered his voice. "There are motives behind that lie you tell, Colón. Every man who was aboard the three ships knows who is the true discoverer. I died a week after we returned to Spain, and you took advantage of my death to accuse me of mutiny so you could claim the discovery. Hernán Pérez Mateo is here to testify to what happened. Tell them, Hernán."

"I am Hernán Pérez Mateo," he began. "I lived and died on the Island of Santo Domingo. And what I say is the truth before God and eternity. I had heard it said that the crew of the *Santa María* conspired to mutiny against Colón. They had lost confidence in Colón, they believed he was unsure of his directions and that they would be lost if they continued with him.

I know for a certainty that when Colón told Pinzón of the possible mutiny, don Martín, without hesitation, responded, 'Señor, hang half-a-dozen of the mutineers on your ship if you believe that is the case. Or throw them into the sea. And, if you are afraid to do so, then I and my brothers will board the *Santa María* and do it for you.

We, the men of Palos and Huelva, proud men of the sea, believe that this fleet which began its voyage under the crown's banner, cannot possibly return without success.' Are those the words of a traitor?" emphasized Pérez Mateo.

Then he continued. "Shaken by his fear of a mutiny, Colón was grateful to Pinzón for calming the crew of the *Santa María*. 'Bienaventurado seásis—good fortune attend you,' Colón told Pinzón on that occasion. Everyone aboard heard him.

The threat of mutiny happened only on Colón's vessel, not on any of the others. The *Santa María's* crew was comprised mostly of men from other places—probably those convicts he spoke about, they were not from Huelva or Palos. All the men in the fleet joked about Colón, some comments about him were more critical and serious than others. Most of them became more disparaging after word got out about his proposal to Pinzón that the quest be abandoned and they should return to Spain.

It is also true that all of us looked to Martín Pinzón for leadership. All of us knew that it was Pinzón who told Colón to alter his course a quarter south because Pinzón was very experienced and adept in nautical matters. In fact, he had observed the passing of many birds of a type that sleep on land at night and go out to sea in the daytime to feed. Pinzón looked at the birds at nightfall, noting the direction of their flight, and he told Colón to change course southwesterly. He knew we were near land!

It is all really a simple matter of logic and truth. The mutiny is a fable. Pinzón's genius and courage led to the discovery. He is the true discoverer. Colón has covered his avarice, cowardice and vaulting ambitions with lies."

It was then that Pinzón spoke up again. "I knew we were close to land," he said. "And I knew we would strike land in three days. I made an arrangement with Colón that if we did not strike land in three days, I would order the men from Palos and Huelva back to Spain, even if it meant my disgrace."

At this, Tlacaellel spoke slowly, but firmly. "The discoverer, if such a claim can be made, is not the one who sighted land from the east. Is that what you are saying? If so, then the discoverer is neither of you, but my Indian forefathers who discovered, settled and died on this land washed by two oceans. This took place thousands of years before any of you ever existed. If there is any truth at all, there is indisputable truth in that! But, let us ask, just for the sake of argument, which of you, Colón or Pinzón, sighted land first?"

Colón jumped, quickly interjecting his claim. In a hurried rush of words he blurted, "I don't care about Pinzón's claim, for him it is a matter of pride to say he is the discoverer. Yes, he suggested a change in course. But I had already determined that. I knew where we were headed at sunset. At 5:30 on the afternoon of October 11, 1492, I ordered every man in the armada to watch for a silhouette of land against the red disk of the setting sun. As usual, all hands had been summoned, and after our evening prayers, we sang the *Salve Regina,* which all seamen sing in their own fashion.

Afterwards, I spoke to the men, reminding them that God had ordained our success and safety. I comforted them, saying that on the morrow they would share with me the greatest discovery of mankind, a round trip route from Europe to the Orient.

I estimated we were 700 leagues from the Canaries,

with fair winds blowing, and land was at hand. I talked to the men and urged them to forget their fears and keep a good watch for the land I knew was there.

To him, who would first sight land, a reward was offered by Their Majesties, Ferdinando and Isabel, who graciously held out a silk doublet and an annual sum of 10,000 maravedís.

My talk finished, my grummet sang out the order to change the watch — 'watch belo-o-w, lay belo-o-w,' he bellowed to the men. During the eleven-and-a-half hours since sunset, a brisk trade wind with a heavy sea blew us at nearly seven knots an hour across the sea.

By dawn, the winds had increased, towing us at nearly nine knots. I made another change of direction over Pinzón's old heading of west-southwest to the original heading we had followed most of the voyage — due west. That was my order — due west. I did it because I wished to make land on a due west course for Japan as I had originally planned. I then . . ."

"Permit me. I am Peralonso Nino. I want to support your claim, Sire, if you would pardon the interruption, please. It was I, *piloto mayor* of the *Santa María,* who advised you against the change to steer due west. I objected. I feared that should we strike land directly in the dark, we would run aground because the shoals and rocks ahead would be invisible in the moonlight. I felt I should speak up now, for my silence would only serve to grace Oblivion's eternal halls."

"Let Colón finish," instructed Tlacaellel. "Continue with your explanation, Colón."

"As I was saying," Colón, hardly perturbed, continued, "I then signaled *Niña* and *Pinta* to follow me due west. All I could think about was the promise I had made the men to turn back if land was not sighted in three days. It was after my signal to proceed west was given that every man on board the three vessels was on his feet in anticipation that our journey was at its end. Some of the boys fell back asleep then, but nobody else could stand the intensity of the moment.

Everyone had his eyes to the west. I heard later that Martín Pinzón complained to his pilot, Cristóbal García, that he did not like carrying sail as we did, in a gale of wind with possible shoals ahead — 'if that crazy Colón can carry sail so can we,' he is said to have remarked in his usual sarcastic manner.

Every man's imagination ran wild. Some thought they could hear waves crashing against a rocky coastline; others claimed to see the white suds of waves swaying along sandy beaches. No one had yet sighted land.

Then, about ten o'clock that night, while standing on the sterncastle, I called Pedro Gutiérrez to confirm what I thought I had seen. 'I saw a light,' I said to Gutiérrez. He peered into the darkness, but so uncertain a thing it was that he did not wish to declare that it was land. Still, he did say he thought he had seen it, too. Rodrigo Sánchez was with us, and he said he saw nothing, for he was not in a position where he could see anything.

The light I saw was like a little wax candle rising and falling. I saw it once or twice more after speaking with Gutiérrez.

'Lumbre! Tierra!' Pedro Yzquierdo, a native of Lepe, yelled out. Whereupon my page-boy, Pedro de Salcedo, shouted back, 'It's already been seen by my master.' In order to protect my claim of having seen the light first, I told Yzquierdo that I had seen and spoken some time ago of that light, which is on the land. Yzquierdo grumbled some obscenity which I let pass because the situation had already created intense feelings on board.

At two o'clock in the morning of October 12, the moon past full and riding high about 70 degrees over Orion on the port quarter, was moving into position to illuminate anything ahead of us. Jupiter could be seen in the east, and Saturn had just set. All eyes were directed on the western horizon, as Deneb neared it.

The stars told us it was two hours past midnight. The *Pinta* was in the lead as we headed at a fast speed toward a destiny which would usher in a new era for mankind.

Antiquity's dying glow remained.

Just then, in the grey of dawn, Rodrigo de Triana, the lookout on *Pinta's* forecastle, peered into the distance and saw a white sand cliff gleaming in the moonlight toward the west.

'Tierra! Tierra!' he shouted. *'Tierra a la vista!* Land ho!' The great moment was at hand.

Martín Pinzón verified Triana's claim and ordered the lombard, already loaded and primed, to be fired as a signal that land had been sighted. He shortened his sail in order to wait for my ship to approach. I could see his men had fallen to their knees on the decks in prayer. In recognition of his effort to verify my claim that I had seen the light in the distance hours before, I called out to Pinzón. 'Señor Pinzón, you have found land,' and Pinzón replied, 'Ay, sir, my reward is not lost.' Quickly, I responded, 'I give you five thousand maravedís as a present.' I reckoned that we were six miles distant to the shore. We sailed around the land I named San Salvador and landed on the west side of what we learned was an island."

"What a remarkable tale you spin, Colón," said Pinzón in a voice filled with disdain and utter disgust. "You mimic Las Casas' words which were written by him to defend your case that you are the discoverer, to wit: 'They all remained affirming, until the night set in, that it was the land they sought, and I certainly believe that it really must have been such, because, according to the route they had followed, all the islands which the Admiral afterwards met with in his second voyage were found in that direction or quarter—towards the southwest.'

Let me tell you what went on among the men of the *Pinta* that night of October 11, 1492. My men congratulated me on setting the armada on the correct course. We doubted that you would honor the person who would sight land. He, who gave the shout of 'tierra a la vista,' was a seaman, Rodrigo de Triana. No doubt he was intoxicated with the everlasting joy of having been chosen by God to earn immortality, and the 10,000 maravedís promised by the Catholic Kings of Castile, Aragon and León to whomever should be so fortunate.

No one can doubt that memorable event, directed by the moon's faint rays, and proven by the sun's later light, that Rodrigo de Triana saw land first.

For shame, Colón, for you to claim before mankind that you had seen a faint light in the middle of a rolling high sea, and to claim that this took place three hours previous to the sighting by Rodrigo. All this tells me about the diminutive stature of your character.

Triana's voice struck hard against your vanity, for it was a voice that sounded like the herald of immortality, and it would certify the attainment of honors, glory, wealth and venerability.

The very moment you heard Rodrigo's voice resounding in the signal of the lombard fired from *Pinta,* your heart sank in despair, for now you could never be the discoverer you had hoped to be. Yes, now you could only be the admiral, the viceroy, and the adelantado by virtue of the contract you formed with the crown of Castile, Aragon and León.

Neither Triana nor myself received any of the reward that you claimed to have shared.

Now I beseech the spirit of Rodrigo de Triana. Come forth, Rodrigo, and speak your mind of that moment in which you were robbed of your rightful reward. Tell us, Rodrigo, of Colón's heritage that began with a lie."

"I am the one who sighted land," spoke Rodrigo de Triana. "I have always been perplexed as to why Colón denied me my just reward. How could he claim he saw land two hours before midnight?

If we were making twelve miles an hour, then in four hours we made forty-eight miles. How could Colón have seen a light made by an Indian from so far away in a rolling sea? Even in daylight, the horizon would not have permitted us to see land from that distance.

Moreover, some say we were fifty-four miles away and that our rate of speed was sometimes as little as three miles an hour, and, they also say, it took us six hours to sight land, not the four claimed by Colón to support his supposed sighting of a fire from such a great distance. It is doubtful that, on that night, he could have seen a light of the highest intensity made by our lighthouses in Europe. The island sits low in the ocean.

I know what Las Casas and Fernando Colón say about the discovery. Fernando tells everyone '*La Pinta* made the signal of land first seen by Rodrigo de Triana, a mariner, and he was not given the 10,000 maravedís reward. It went to the Admiral, who first saw a light in the shadows of the coming night, an indication of the spiritual light introduced by him in those evening mists.'"

Rodrigo de Triana paused for a moment. Then he said, "I've been robbed of my place in history. I have been cheated of my place in society during my life. My children's children have been despoiled of the richness of their human heritage. Colón, know this, I journeyed throughout Spain trying to get support for my cause. I suffered poverty, ridicule and shame, for no one would believe my claim. I suffered much disapointment and many hardships because of the reward I did not receive. It would have eased my life and that of my children.

Colón, because of you and your greed I renounced Christianity and went to live in Africa where I converted to Islam. You, who sign your name Cristo Ferens — Christ Bearer — know ye now, your life has been as much a fraud as is your name. If you think it not a fraud, then explain to me how it is not."

When he had finished speaking, a din, like plaintive voices resounding in a great hall, could be heard in the forest. The debate continued deep into the night. It was the night the spirits had stilled for a single, eternal moment.

Chapter 8

Jicaque Land Revisited

Meanwhile, Quilaztli, still in the Archives of the Indies, began to work on the documents presented by Tilini. On one of the ten tables were eight bundles of documents, each consisting of one thousand pages. Trembling with anticipation, Quilaztli loosed the bow of the ebony colored ribbon which bound the first bundle.

The title page of the documents read, *INDICE DE LOS PAPELES DEL CONSEJO DE INDIAS* — Index of the Papers of the Council of the Indies.

Quietly, Quilaztli ran his finger down the list of documents as if studying the calligraphy. Suddenly, he stopped. He took a quick gulp of air, almost as if he were choking. A group of words jumped out at him — *Information and Testimony Concerning How the Admiral and*

Those who were with him Discovered the Main-Land, 1493-96. Quilaztli read on, his head spinning as if in a vortex, his breathing laborious but now steady.

"On board the *Niña,*" he whispered, "another name for the caravel *Santa Clara,* on Thursday, June 12, 1494 . . . the very magnificent Sire, don Cristóbal Colón, Admiral of the Ocean Sea, viceroy and Governor in perpetuity of the Island of San Salvador, and of the other isles and Mainland discovered and to be discovered . . . on the second voyage for the said admiral. Be it declared:—"

"Be it declared —." *What's this?* thought Quilaztli. He turned the pages and found various lists of mariners and ships that had sailed between 1493 and 1502.

"These are incomplete lists of some of the men who were with Colón on his second, third and fourth voyages," interjected Tilini, impatiently. "Think, Quilaztli," thundered Tilini as the monkey on his shoulder fidgeted in an attempt to keep its balance. "Remember the day in 1502 when you first saw Colón on the coast that the Jicaque called Maia. Do any of these names mean anything to you?"

Quilaztli nodded his head in the affirmative, looked up at Tilini and then at the long lists of names. He began to read:

"Francisco Niño of Moguer, pilot of the *Niña*

Alonso Medel of Palos, ship master

Juan de la Cosa, resident of Puerto de Santa María
of Santona, cartographer and mariner"

Here is one with no first name listed, he thought,
Morón of Moguer, mariner.

He continued to read the Archives list aloud, his voice echoing throughout the hall which now took on an eerie ambiance resembling the scene of the Azteca tribunal in the forest.

"Francisco de Lepe of Moguer, mariner
Diego Beltrán of Moguer, mariner
Domingo Genoves, no status
Estefano Veneciano, no status
Juan de España, a Basque
Gómez, no first name, a ship's caulker from Palos
Ramiro Pérez from Lepe
Mateo Morales from Ceuta
Juan del Puerto, no status
Gonzalo Vizcaíno, ship's boy
Alonso de Huelva, ship's boy ...."

The roll call revealed a hierarchy in the Spanish ship that had sailed to the land of the Jicaque. Through Tilini, Quilaztli learned more about the Spaniards and their titles. Despite their rudeness, Quilaztli realized that the crew was as well-organized as the social order from which they came. He realized that the Europeans could not be defeated. The admiral of the Ocean Sea was not a king, but he was part of a great hierarchy that would spread its tentacles to all the reaches of the world. The metaphor of the ship as a microcosm of Spanish colonialism became clear to Quilaztli. The men on the ship represented much more than a list of names.

Aside from their technology, their organization and ability to communicate across vast distances made them invincible. Quilaztli looked at the titles among the crewmen with intense interest. A *capitán mercante* or ship master like Alonso Medel, he learned, was the captain of the ship who assured the vessel operated as it should, making all assignments for proper operation and navigation. All this was not unlike the war-captains among the Aztecs, Mayans, Incas and others. But what made Quilaztli tremble with apprehension about the Europeans was the fact that they had a title for every task. In addition, they could communicate not only across distances, but across time because they had a written word. To remind them of the details, the king's archives were filled with diaries, reports and correspondence that described the Americas and its peoples ... just like the ones he presently was reading.

For the moment, Quilaztli turned back to the ship's crew. He was most intrigued by the role of the *piloto may-*

or, or pilot. Specially trained, the pilot was the navigator of the ship. He communicated directly with the captain. He kept a navigator's diary with information about the direction, distance and time of travel of his ship in relation to latitude, and, as best as it could be reckoned, longitude.

Each day at noon, the pilot gave a written report to his captain regarding the route of the ship as well as their present location. As navigator, he was in charge of lanterns and flags used as semaphores or signals to seamen on other ships when it was necessary to communicate any changes in direction or speed. He also kept the ship's hour-glass to determine time and distance. The *piloto mayor* was required to keep the ship's official navigational charts and other maps. A good navigator also advised on the winds and the condition of the sea as well as its depth near the coast lines. He was the ship's memory, for he could tell with documented accuracy whether the ship had been in certain waters before, and he could backtrack on the guideless sea. Finally, at night he served as the ship's eye.

The *contramaestre,* or boatswain, concluded Quilaztli, outranked the ordinary seamen in the same way that a sergeant outranks soldiers. Such a person used a whistle to sound certain signals with which to communicate with the seamen the actual instructions to assure the operation of a ship as ordered by the shipmaster.

Quilaztli was surprised to learn that most of the

ship's boys, or *pajes de escoba,* were between eight and fourteen years of age. Usually, they signed on a ship to learn about seamanship under the tutelage of an experienced shipmaster. They served as errand boys, valets, and generally tended to sweeping and cleaning the ship at sea.

Quilaztli's curiosity led him to the word *calafate,* or caulker, for there were several of them. In this area, he learned that the large wooden ships could not float unless they were made watertight, a time-consuming job. The caulker constantly sealed the ship with tar or oakum, making sure every crack or hole was plugged against the powers of the sea.

In his review, Quilaztli also noticed that the word "mariner" appeared on the list frequently. Because there were so many of them, he assumed correctly that a *marinero* was an ordinary seaman. As laborers, they did all the actual work on the ship, including hoisting the sails, lowering or raising the anchor, assisting the caulker, or loading and unloading the ship. Often, one of them, assisted by several seamen, was the ship's cook. In times of danger, the *marineros* also served to defend the ship by manning small arms and artillery.

The roll call reverberated through time as Quilaztli's voice took on a martial tone.

"Francisco Genoves from Córdoba

Rodrigo Mobuer from Moguer
Rodrigo, no last name, from Cartaya, a ship caulker
Alonso Niño from Moguer
Juan Vizcaíno, no status
Bartolomé Pérez from Rota, pilot
of the second ship, *San Juan*
Alonso Pérez Roldán from Malaga,
ship master of the *San Juan*
Sebastián de Ayamonte, mariner
Francisco Calvo from Moguer, mariner
Fernando Martín Gutiérrez from Palos, mariner
Juan Albarrasque of Puerto de Santa María, mariner
Nicolás Estefano from Mallorca, mariner
Cristóbal Vivas from Moguer, ship's boy
Rodrigo Santander from Moguer, ship's boy
Juan García of Ucas, ship's boy
Hernando López from Huelva, ship's boy
Cristóbal Pérez Niño from Palos,
shipmaster of the caravel *Cardera*"

Quilaztli froze. It was the next name. He knew the man. It was Fermín Genoves, the boatswain. *It was Genoves,* remembered Quilaztli. *It was he who called me an hechicero — a warlock.*

And this next name, Gonzalo Alonso Galleote from Huelva, a mariner. He is the one who laughed at me and said, "Hechicero, can you tell me what the future holds for your people?"

In anger, now, Quilaztli squinted his eyes and he spied the next name, Juan de Jerez of Moguer, mariner. *He's the one who contemptuously yelled, "Can you show us how to make gold from these wretched stones that fill your land?"*

I did not know then what your words meant, he thought, *but I do now.*

Tilini's transparent form hovered over Quilaztli as he read the last few names on the page.

I must finish reading all these names, so I can know what I must know, Quilaztli thought.

Slowly, he whispered each name as the sound of his voice bounced off the heavy stone walls.

"Francisco Carral from Palos, mariner
Juan Griego, from Genova, mariner
Alonso Pérez from Huelva, mariner
Juan Vizcaíno from Cartaya, mariner
Cristóbal Lorenzo of Palos, ship's boy
Francisco de Medina from Moguer, ship's boy
Guillermo, no last name, from Palos, ship's boy
Diego Leal from Moguer, no status given
Francisco Niño from Palos, ship's boy and
Tristán, no last name, from Valduerna, ship's boy"

As if he had been at back-breaking labor for hours,

and now soaking in streaming perspiration, Quilaztli murmured, "At last. At last I know the names of those who laughed at me in the land of the Jicaque in the Christian year of 1502." Then, with venom in his voice, Quilaztli added, "I will curse that day forever." He bowed his head as if in prayer, but he was thinking: *So these are the so-called discoverers and conquerors of the Río de la Posesión — the River Where Possession was Taken. Well, now we will see who possesses whom.*

Chapter 9

The Contract

The winds of the forest had stopped their whispering. There was a certain solitude in the stillness of that instant. If one could have caught a glimpse of that eternal moment, he would have heard the voices of the tribunal begin anew. The thick forest canopy gave the voices a muffled character. Up close, the sound of voices could be heard with singular clarity. The smell of death was all around the ancient Azteca shrine. The eerie, pulsating light from eternity's beacon glowed and dimmed, glowed and dimmed. In the span of an ocelot's wink, eternity's past, present and future occupied the same space.

"Colón has lied about everything, especially in regard to the first voyage," shouted Pinzón in anger. Still, the Azteca tribunal had the responsibility to evaluate whether he had lied about the circumference of the earth, about the mutiny, and about his role in sighting land. These were crucial matters in the effort to determine whether Colón was a liar or a victim of circumstances. Was deceit and deception innate to Colón's character? Damning was the testimony against Colón. The tribunal wanted to hear more.

"Tell us, Pinzón," asked Tlacaellel, "do you have any written proof that Colón deliberately sought to perpetrate a fraud on the men who sailed with him, and then on the crown of Spain?"

Pinzón was whispering. "All that has been said here," he began, "is testimony to that point. Some of it has been presented as documented proof of Colón's scheming to commit a fraud on everyone so he could get his way. But, and listen to this, there are two documents that have not been discussed here. The first involves the fake logs that Colón kept on the voyage. And the second is the *Capitulaciones* — the contract—given him by Ferdinando and Isabel, our Catholic Kings. Ask Cristóbal García, the *piloto mayor* of the *Santa Maria,* about the fake logs."

"Cristóbal García, come forth!" shrieked Caudi. "Come forth from the bowels of purgatory where you have been condemned before your soul can be redeemed." The shimmering, ghostly form of Cristóbal García appeared instantaneously in a clatter of chains and moans of pain. García had led a hard life. But, at the same time, he had been a part of the lie that had hurt so many. Indeed, it was Cristóbal García, himself, who knew more about Colón's logs than anyone else.

"Speak! Speak!" yelled Caudi to the ghost of García. "It is the only way to your redemption. Tell the tribunal about the fake logs."

Moaning and trembling, the voice of García began with a single word: "Lies," he said. "They are all lies which can never be taken back and a hundred more have been spoken and written to cover the first one.

I know. I know because it is I who helped Colón prepare the fake logs of the first voyage. He had his reasons. Yes, Colón deliberately faked one of the log books and kept an accurate one for his own information so that only he would know how far the ships had traveled.

He told me to prepare the fake log because he wished to alleviate the men's fears that they were getting too far from land in a sea only Alonso Sánchez had known. I recall in mid-September 1492, the eleventh day, to be exact, the men of the *Santa María* asked Colón how far they had traveled. He told them they had traveled only sixteen leagues when in fact we had traveled twenty leagues on that day. I know because I had prepared the chart as Colón had instructed me to do. The men knew he was lying to them. They knew how to reckon distance as well. That is why they threatened to mutiny against him. Yes, it was Pinzón who came aboard. He stopped the mutiny from happening. Only the men of the *Santa María* had been deceived by Colón. The men of the *Niña* and the *Pinta* knew approximately how far they had sailed."

Colón had heard the damning testimony of Cristóbal García, and, as soon as he could, he responded with his views. "Yes, I did give the men a reduced mileage estimate, but who could know what the true distance was? The problem lay with the inaccuracy of our equipment.

No one can accurately measure east-west distances at sea. Even if I had used an hour glass, the motion of the ship upon the waves would have resulted in a distortion of time. I had to guess at the speed we were making. Whenever a piece of driftwood, or seaweed, floated by, we attempted to time its passage from one end of the ship to the other. Sometimes we threw something over the prow and watched it float aft.

I used dead reckoning like anyone else. All I did was lay out a compass course and estimate the distance traveled on my chart. García knew that. There was much room for error. Besides, as the commander of the expedition, it was my prerogative to tell the men what I thought best for them to know. Ironically, as it turned out, the fake log was more accurate than the one I had been using for the actual estimation of distance. On September 11, 1492, sixteen leagues was more accurate than twenty leagues."

"The question here," countered Pinzón in a booming tone of voice, "is not the result. No. The question is the intent to defraud your crew, Colón. Yes, you. Your fake logs were aimed at concealing the lie you told Their Majesties.

I know that before the first voyage you were able to convince them that the earth was smaller in circumference because you knew they would approve a shorter trip than the one necessary to circumnavigate the earth.

I opine that you would have used the fake log to prove you right and thereby get Their Majesties to approve future trips. But later, why did you lie to your men? Our men knew just about how far we had traveled. For their morale, they should have known what we knew."

Confident and imperious in tone and manner, Colón concluded: "A commander has his prerogatives. If I, as you say, defrauded King Ferdinando and Queen Isabel, then they gained more than I. They gained an empire!

I have nothing more to say on that matter." With this, Colón fell silent.

"Appear before us, Juan de Coloma," commanded Tleume.

Like Cristóbal García, Coloma appeared before the tribunal. But, unlike García, Coloma's appearance was serene. His life on earth had been gentler, for he had served in Their Majesties' court since he was a teenager.

"I am Juan de Coloma, personal clerk and notary of King Ferdinando and Queen Isabel. I know why I have been summoned, and I am prepared to give a full account of the Capitulations made to Colón by Their Highnesses. In regard to the first voyage, I was there on April 17, 1492 at Santa Fe de la Vega de Granada, and it was I who transcribed the Capitulations at the request of my Sovereign Lords."

"Would you present us with the literal wording of the Capitulations so that all of us may know the intent of Ferdinando and Isabel?" asked Copil.

"I am pleased to do so as best as I can recall," replied Coloma. He then began a recitation of Colón's contract with the king and queen of Spain.

"The things supplicated and which Your Highnesses give and declare to Cristóbal Colón in some satisfaction for what he has discovered in the Ocean Sea, and for the voyage which now, with the aid of God, he is about to make therein, are as follows:

First. That Your Highnesses as Lords that are of said oceans, make from this time the said don Cristóbal Colón your admiral in all those islands and mainland which by his hand and industry maybe discovered or acquired in the said oceans, during his life and after his death, his heirs and successors, from one to another perpetually, with all the preeminences and prerogatives belonging to the said office and according as don Alonso Henriques, your High Admiral of Castile, and his predecessors in the said office held it in their districts.

I signed — It so pleases Their Highnesses. Juan de Coloma.

Likewise, that Your Highnesses make the said don Cristóbal Colón your viceroy land Governor General in all the said islands and mainland which, as has been said, he may discover or acquire in the said seas; and that for the government of each one and of any one of them he may make selection of three persons for each office, and that Your Highnesses may choose and select the one who shall be most serviceable to you, and thus the lands which our Lord shall permit him to discover and acquire will be better governed in the service of Your Highnesses.

I signed—It so pleases Their Highnesses. Juan de Coloma.

Item: that all and whatever merchandise, whether it be pearls, precious stones, gold, silver, spices, and other things whatsoever, and merchandise of whatever kind, name and manner it may be, which may be bought, bartered, discovered, acquired or obtained within the limits of the said Admiralty, Your Highnesses grant henceforth to the said don Cristóbal Colón, and will that he may have and take for himself, the tenth part of all of them, deducting all the expenses which may be incurred therein; so that of what shall remain free and clear, he may have and take the tenth part for himself, and do therewith as he will, the other nine parts remaining for Your Highnesses.

I signed — it so pleases Their Highnesses. Juan de Coloma.

Likewise, that if on account of the merchandise

that he might bring from the said islands and mainland, which as aforesaid he shall acquire and discover, or of that which may be taken in exchange for the same from other merchants, any suit shall arise in the place where the said trade and traffic shall be held and conducted; and if by the preeminence of his office of Admiral it may belong to him to take cognizance of the said suit, and thus it is decreed henceforth.

I signed — It so pleases Their Highnesses. Juan de Coloma.

It so pleases Their Highnesses if it belongs to the said office of the Admiral, as the said Admiral don Alonso Henríques held it and the others, his predecessors in their districts, and if it be just.

I signed — Juan de Coloma.

Item: that in all the vessels which may be equipped for the said traffic and negotiation each time and whensoever and as often as they may be equipped, the said Admiral don Cristóbal Colón may, if he wishes, contribute and pay the eighth part of all that may be spent in the equipment. And also that he may have and take of the profit, the eighth part of all which may result from such equipment.

I signed — It so pleases Their Highnesses. Juan de Coloma.

These capitulations are executed and dispatched with the responses of Your Highnesses at the end of each article in the town of Santa Fe de la Vega de Granada on the 17th day of April in the Year of the Nativity of Our Lord Jesus Christ, 1492.

Yo, el Rey Yo, la Reina

By order of the King and Queen, I signed — Juan de Coloma.

Registered. Coloma."

After the recitation of the contract, Yoanizi, who had sat quietly for so long, was the first to speak. "What does it mean," he asked, "when in the first article it reads 'The things supplicated and which Your Highnesses give and declare to Cristóbal Colón in some satisfaction for what he has discovered in the Ocean Sea?' Is that an acknowledgement that Colón had already made a claim before he had even set sail, or does it mean that he made other discoveries in the Ocean Sea that the European world did not yet know?"

"I must confess," responded Coloma, "that when I first heard those words I did not know what to make of them either. I did puzzle over them and concluded that the words were designed to cover Colón's conclusions that lands may be found beyond the Ocean Sea as we knew it. Perhaps, Colón was buoyed by the fact that he knew Alonso Sánchez had made discoveries beyond the Sargasso Sea and that he was confident that he would confirm them — nay, claim them as his discovery."

"I submit to you," interrupted Pinzón with some force in his voice, "that very phrase shows that Colón knew of Alonso Sánchez's discoveries, for he had stolen that man's charts and then sought to defraud Their Majesties with information he knew to be a sure thing. What more do you need to hear? The fake logs tell much about Colón as a habitual liar, and the Capitulations tell how far he was willing to go to satisfy his vaulting ambitions.

The Capitulations spell out the motives. Colón wanted to establish a *mayorazgo* — an entail of money and property — for his descendants. Such a *mayorazgo* would make him one of the most powerful and wealthiest of men in all the known world!"

"I, too, am perplexed about the points you raise, Pinzón," Copil spoke up. "I am also perplexed, as well, about what rights Ferdinando and Isabel thought they had that they could give away that which was not theirs. Is it possible to summon their royal majesties before us?"

"Ferdinando cannot be summoned, for he is still among the living. But Isabel is among us," explained Tleume.

"I protest her presence." Juan de Coloma voiced his opinion. "For this is a most undignified gathering. I have known the queen since her birth. I have known of her goodness. She is a saint, and Rome has not been loath to beatify her. Her subjects throughout the realm recognized her purity. She was no ordinary mortal. Once, after she had emerged from the Alcazar of Segovia, with my own eyes, I saw the people fall to their knees in her presence. Such inner beauty has not been seen on earth in centuries. I beseech you, spirits, not to permit her here."

To this, Caudi responded, "What Coloma says is true, but in the interests of truth we can spare no measure, we must put at risk our very being."

"I warn you, if she is summoned, you may incur the wrath of the Creator," announced Tleume, "for she is a

'Chosen One.' You will be careful of her treatment, and the manner in which you address her presence, for the Creator has especially blessed her existence. To ensure our protection against the wrath of the Creator, only Caudi and I will be permitted to speak with her. You may hear her answers and be content with that."

Having thus spoken, Tleume waved his scepter and, in an instant, Queen Isabel was among them.

Her bearing was beyond imagination. Isabel, once the stately, young monarch of Spain and its empire, emanated a powerful presence.

Like her subjects at Segovia, the Azteca tribunal felt as if their bodies lay prostrated on the forest floor.

Colón, Pinzón, and their followers could not view her, as the intensity of the light radiating from her defied all laws of the universe. Like Tilini, Tleume and Caudi, Isabel was wrapped in a transparent, ethereal airiness filled with crescent moons, falling stars, and mysterious planetary-like spheres never before seen. When she spoke, it was with a voice as soft and gentle as a mist in a spring dawn.

"What is it you wish with me?" she intoned.

Tleume spoke. "Queen Isabel, I ...."

"Please, do not call me Queen," she countered quickly, "for there are no kings and queens in the presence of the Creator. You may call me Isabel."

"Isabel," began Tleume anew. "We are gathered here to determine certain truths which may guide the mortal Quilaztli in his quest to rid the world of injustice. We therefore humbly ask your presence and supplicate your indulgence of the many queries we must ask of you. May we ask certain questions of you that may point the way to truth?"

"You may. Please ask your first question."

"In your earthly life, by what right did you make your claim to lands discovered by Colón?"

Isabel replied without hesitation. "The right of claim is inherent in European culture, as is the concept of the divine right of kings. Since time immemorial, all European nations have claimed lands through war, declaration and colonization.

As a mortal, I will admit, I succumbed to European tradition. But I went a step further. I defended the rights of natives to live as members of the civilized world. I decried their enslavement, and I began work toward the recognition of legal rights for natives.

Spain's right to claim was blessed by Pope Alexander VI who was the Vicar of Christ on Earth, and, at Tordesillas, the Portuguese and Spanish crowns submitted their rightful claims to Rome in 1493.

To complete my answer to you, assumed sovereignty was the first step to the European claim. Then, colonization ensured rightful possession.

Am I right to assume that your next question treats of the Capitulations signed at Santa Fe de la Vega?"

"Yes, Isabel." Tleume spoke in measured tones. "But more precisely, what role did Cristóbal Colón play in the writing of his contract?"

"Colón, in his presentations, had convinced Ferdinando and me that he could and would discover a route to India. He had information no one else had, to the best of our knowledge.

Please remember, we were at the end of our siege of Granada. Victory was within our grasp as we ensured that our claim to Spain, by war and treaty, would be recognized by the Moors and their Islamic leaders. Now, we felt, we could turn our energies to another enterprise. Colón approached with assurances that he knew of lands that existed in the Ocean Sea. He needed us to endorse and protect what he was about to do.

For our part, we assumed that he had seen what he said he would claim in our names.

That may explain the strange words at the beginning of the document.

At the time, I felt that if Colón wanted our protection to new claims that he would make in our names, then we should certainly not take the chance Colón would establish his own claim to lands discovered before our signing of the contract.

As shrewd mortals, which we thought ourselves to be, we chose to legally bind all we could in order to avoid an adverse claim later from Colón.

As you can now see, the idea was to make the contract as inclusive and as much to our advantage as possible."

"If I may," interjected Caudi, "I would ask about the hereditary items in the contract. Hereditary items, mind you. How could this man, Cristóbal Colón, possibly deserve such concessions?"

"It is true that Colón was an outsider to our Spanish interests. Still, like any other vassal, he was subject to our prerogatives. Therefore, if he hoped to gain our support, then he must make concessions. If he made them, then it was within our power to grant hereditary titles. Titles were at the proper disposal of kings and queens. They were our concessions, so to speak."

"True," said Tleume, "but you went beyond the mere granting of one title in perpetuity, that of admiral. You went on to grant the additional titles of viceroy and governor. These, too, were granted in perpetuity."

"In the Capitulations," came the reply, "we recognized his leadership needs by way of a title for the expedition. Colón was not content with that and petitioned us to reconsider his just reward for his proposed discoveries. That is why, on April 30, 1492, by decree, as was our prerogative, we amended his contract.

Lest history doubt my words, I quote from the decree as follows: 'It is our will and pleasure that you, the said Cristóbal Colón, after you have discovered and acquired the said islands and mainland in the said Ocean Sea, or any of them whatsoever, shall be our admiral of the said islands and mainland which you thus discover and acquire and shall be our viceroy and governor therein, and shall be empowered from that time forward to call and entitle yourself don Cristóbal Colón, and that your children and successors in the said office and charge may likewise entitle and call themselves don, and admiral and viceroy thereof.'

Ferdinando and I felt that Colón, as our discoverer and our admiral, should govern in our place that which he had discovered. We further confirmed our royal wishes in another decree issued in Barcelona on May 23, 1493, thus our agreement was blessed twice, once in Santa Fe de la Vega, and again in Barcelona, after the signing of the Treaty of Tordesillas. We further extended our prerogative to recognize his title and claim after his second voyage which took place between 1493 and 1496, in which he made new discoveries."

At this, Caudi asked, somewhat impatiently, "Why and how were you able to give Colón such latitude to lands and people you have never seen, and ...?"

"Let me interrupt you, if I may," said Isabel. "One has to understand that all of Europe had an interest in India, the Spice Islands and the Orient. As long ago as the expeditions of Marco Polo, his father and uncle in the thirteenth century, Europeans felt the need to find a route there. It was also theorized that not all of the earth had been claimed, just like Africa.

Our claim was based on the notion that the uncivilized world was there for the taking. Our prerogatives did not extend to assuming sovereignty over another great lord's territory.

Thus, the territorial extent of Colón's rights coincided with the claim he had made in our name. We owned the land and distributed rights and privileges to it. His contract read, 'all the islands and mainland which by his hand and industry may be discovered or acquired in the said Ocean Sea,' signified that our claim would extend as far as Colón, his lieutenants or anyone we may appoint had gone. In each case, we did so contractually."

"We who are present have doubted the integrity of

Colón," spoke Tleume. "I do not wish nor intend any offense, but we are curious to know if, at any time in the negotiations, you felt that Colón was untrustworthy, or that he intended to commit fraud against the crown of Spain."

"First, I must say, I take no offense at your inquiry. We had the utmost trust in Colón. He had been highly recommended to us by several people, including the Duque de Medinacelli as well as my confessor, Fray Antonio Marchena. True, Colón did join us in the fight against the infidel. No, we had no reason to distrust him. Aside from his proposal in which we reasoned we had nothing to lose if we sponsored him, we also felt that he had much to risk, accidentally, should he fail in his quest, and legally, by contract, should his intentions be illegal.

All that Colón received from us in the Capitulations and the subsequent royal decrees was the post of viceroy and governor general of the lands discovered, with the right to nominate others for appointment to office. I can assure you that this is true.

These same concessions were extended to his direct and rightful heirs. In addition to those titles he and his heirs were granted the right to derive monetary compensation at the rate of one-tenth of our profits from trade and production in the newly discovered lands.

Further, he was to receive one-eighth of the profits of any expedition to which he may invest from his own pocket, and, as admiral, he could claim as much as one third of the profits taken in combat as a perquisite of his office.

As viceroy, he could derive money from the nominations for appointments to political offices in the newly discovered lands.

These concessions are, with exception, not unusual, they are customary. My High Admiral of Castile, Alonso Henríquez, likewise had received similar concessions in our war against Islam."

Caudi interjected a question. "Was this grant made without restrictions, either to Colón or his heirs?"

"There were restrictions," answered Isabel, "and there were limitations. An unrestricted grant to Colón's economic and governmental powers would have established Colón and his heirs as an independent monarchy. That was not our intent. By limiting Colón and his heirs to those concessions that I have mentioned, we thereby maintained our rights as sovereigns, should he be unable to keep order in his dominions as viceroy. There are implied restrictions to the titles we conferred on him.

For example, a viceroy is nothing more than our representative. Should he fail in his duties, our intervention would come in the form of an investigation, his removal, if warranted, and our prerogative to grant a redress of grievances to those injured by his incompetence."

This time, it was Tleume who interjected, "So, if I may indulge your comment a little further, there did exist some doubt about Colón ....?"

"The crown seeks to protect itself from all situations," Isabel responded. "True, Colón's contract was no exception. Any doubts the crown harbored about Colón were part of negotiating an advantageous position for us.

Naturally, the purpose of the contract was to place safeguards against possible fraud and to set up a defense of our interests in this enterprise.

Any violation of his titles and the responsibilities attached to them, we naturally would construe to be a violation of his contract. Our lawyers could quickly and easily throw a cloud over any of his claims, provided that the violations were true and we adjudged him to be unsuitable.

If our interests, and the public's, were threatened by his intentions, the situation would demand such action be taken. That was our providential and legal position. But do not misconstrue my answer to suit your needs. A contract is meant to regulate relationships between consenting parties in any given enterprise. Our relationship with Colón was purely one of business. He was not necessarily one of our court favorites."

"Still," commented Caudi, "given all that you have

said, it seems that Colón's share was disproportionate to what the crown was to receive.

Furthermore," added Caudi, "I calculate that by adding one-eighth, one-tenth and one-third, Colón could have possibly collected over one-half of the profits! It seems unlikely that you, and Ferdinando, would have agreed to that."

"We did object," she quickly replied, "to the one third share of his admiralty entitlement. But, initially, we did not object to it until Colón expanded his demand to include an additional one-third of the lands in the newly discovered territories.

Given such a demand, we had to deny him any additional claims.

Furthermore, after our lawyers had reviewed his admiralty entitlement, we found grounds to deny the applicability of his demanded entitlement as admiral to one-third of the riches he may find. This was because we had never intended for him to claim booty obtained in military expeditions against the natives of the New World.

The entitlement worked well for Admiral Henríquez when he fought against the Moors and pirates in our Holy War against Islam, but it clashed with our policy to protect the natives of the New World. Indeed, upon his return from his first voyage, when Colón presented me with Indian slaves, I challenged him by asking, 'by what right do you take my vassals as slaves?' Colón had no response.

Perhaps, those words expressed the first statement made by any European power that concerned a New World Indian policy. In the absence of clear language in the contract, we, as situations evolved, sought to define our position and intentions in the entire enterprise."

Cutting off the exchange, Tleume said, "We are satisfied with your responses, Isabel, and we thank you most graciously for your presence."

Then, as quickly as she had appeared, Isabel disappeared.

With Isabel no longer present, it was Copil who first spoke. "We are dumbfounded at her responses. We find it totally incomprehensible that such a contract, by her own words and her own admission, and which was based on the mistrust of two consenting parties who then agreed to forcefully take what was not theirs, was the basis of our demise as a people."

There was silence. No one responded to Copil's comment. Instead, the stillness in the forest deepened.

Chapter 10

The Columbus Curse

Quilaztli instantaneously knew all that had occurred in the forest. He hoped to find a way to punish Colón, but he knew not how.

His mind vacillated between the proceedings in the forest and the present urge of the task that was before him to learn all that was in the archives.

How, he asked himself, *can that which has been heard in the forest relate to these documents that describe events that happened in the future?*

Just then, Tilini waved his scepter and seven bundles of documents appeared before Quilaztli. Each bundle contained the usual one-thousand pages.

A quick inspection revealed to Quilaztli that the first bundle was labeled, *"Sección Patronato, legajo 8,"* and the last one was *"Sección Patronato, legajo 14."*

He dusted off the first bundle, removed the ribbon around it, and opened its cover.

For a moment, Quilaztli sat stunned. Again he read the words of the first page. They seemed unbelievable.

Mouthing the words aloud, he read, "*CRISTOBAL COLON Y SUS DESCENDIENTES Y LOS PLEITOS DE ESTOS CON LA CORONA* — Cristóbal Colón and his descendants and their case against the crown."

Quilaztli learned that for several years after the discovery of the New World, Colón had ridden the crest of Fortune's wave. Hailed as viceroy and admiral of the Ocean Sea, he enjoyed the broadest of political powers bestowed upon him by the crown.

He also learned that, in 1496, Colón had directed his brother, Bartolomé, to found the city of Santo Domingo on the island of Hispaniola. It was to become the capital of the colony.

Colón, aside from his share of the royal revenues, including large amounts of gold panned from the river sands of Hispaniola, also collected his one-eighth investments in the various expeditions in which he had participated. But all did not fare well for Colón.

Quilaztli learned of the fate of the Colón dynasty. He turned the pages slowly. Tears of a profound sadness filled his eyes, for the knowledge he had gained could not reverse the force of a history that doomed his people to a living oblivion.

Chapter 11

The New World Chroniclers

In an instant, Quilaztli was back in the forest. The mist that rose from the ground gave the trees an eerie appearance. In his out-of-body state, Quilaztli could barely make out the remains of the dead Aztec priests with whom he had begun this journey into the past and future.

He could see his own body lying in its own excrement. And, he could see the Aztec tribunal, their faces gaunt, their eyes dull and lifeless. Their bodies had been contorted, as when they had fallen in the stupor of their present condition. Like Quilaztli, they, too, were cognizant of the vision they had experienced.

"Tell us," spoke Copil, "What have you learned from your odyssey into the future?"

Quilaztli could see the faces of those who sat around the tribunal in the forest. Some were friends, others foes. Yet they all had an interest in his response. Peering at them through the mist, Quilaztli spoke.

"Tonight," he began, "I read many documents, enough to fill all of the palaces at Tenochtitlan and all of the pyramids built by the ancient Mayas, Toltecas, Zapotecas and Olmecas. I read through so many documents that all the fortified palaces of the Incas would not be enough to hold them.

The European colonials, unleashed by Colón's voyage, have a written word which they placed on paper to remind them about all the details of what they had seen, from the first day to the last. They have put these papers in archives.

Their archives are filled with diaries, reports and correspondence that describe the land, the resources, the animals, the plants and the people of what they call 'the New World.'

We have our oral traditions, but they form only a collective memory. They have a written tradition that lasts forever and preserves the clarity of their past. With their written works they can study the past and predict the future, as the Maya did with the science of astronomy. With their written works, they can preserve truth or falsehood and protect themselves from all who would dare to slander them. But, from them I have learned much about our future. I have come a step closer to the truth."

Tlacaellel spoke. "How can truth be falsified from those documents that preserve the clarity of their past?"

"Perhaps I spoke somewhat simply about their written traditions," Quilaztli replied. "In many instances, it is their truth as they saw it.

But I also learned that lies can be placed on paper, and so, too, the truth that many of them may contain can also be reinterpreted to support the causes in other writings.

This has been the case with the chroniclers who later wrote the defenses and justifications of Colón's claim to the New World."

"Who are these chroniclers, or masters of deceit, who have played so treacherously with truth?" asked Yoanizi.

"There are so many, I know not where to begin," replied Quilaztli. "But let me tell you about some of them, for I have divided the groups into two main categories — the Colombinistas, and the Anti-Colombinistas.

The Colombinistas are those who have interpreted the truth in order to defend the New World claims of Colón and his family.

The Anti-Colombinistas have attacked and opposed

the claims of Colón, as evidenced in their writings.

Between the two there may be some truth, for the Colombinistas have attempted to fortify their truths by creating confusion between the mortal man and the legend. It was a legend that sprang from the worship of Colón as a hero. The Anti-Colombinistas, on the other hand, have attacked the legend and the man. They have wanted to show that Colón was not the genius he has been made out to be.

The first of the Colombinistas is .... "

"Before you give us their names," interrupted Yoanizi, "tell us more about how they fit into the written tradition of the Europeans—how did they come into being?"

Quilaztli thought for a moment, then spoke. "As far as I have been able to ascertain, the origins of the Colombinistas and Anti-Colombinistas can be traced to a time soon after the voyage of discovery when Colón's claim was challenged by his detractors.

It began with a series of legal controversies in which Colón and his descendants defended the claim of discovery and the estate that issued from it.

The controversies surfaced when, after 1496, the Spanish sovereigns, Ferdinando and Isabel, began a series of legal maneuvers to review the agreement made by them with Colón at Santa Fe de Granada in 1492. That agreement was made before he had embarked on his first voyage of discovery.

However, the vagaries of the *Capitulaciones*, the 1492 contract, proved impossible to interpret when it was realized that the vast and wealthy lands he had discovered were not the Indies he had sought. Furthermore, the complaints and accusations made by the Spanish settlers about Colón's mismanagement of the colony at Hispaniola cost him the political prerogatives granted in the agreement of 1492.

By the time of his death in 1506, Colón's petitions to the crown had been unresolved, and he had fallen into disfavor."

"Yes, but who were the earliest of the pro-Colón writers?" asked Copil. "Were they members of his own family?"

"Precisely," responded Quilaztli. "Fernando Colón, illegitimate son of the Discoverer, and a family friend by the name of Fray Bartolomé de las Casas, set the rhythm and tempo of the Colombinistas who were to follow.

Fernando Colón, who, to me, appeared to be a man of great intellectual curiosity, wrote the biography of his father, *Historia del almirante Don Cristóbal Colón en la cual se da particular y verdadera relación de su vida y de sus hechos y del descubrimiento de las Indias Occidentales llamadas Nuevo-Mundo.*

Fernando was born in the summer of 1488 in Cordoba. His peasant mother was Beatriz Enríquez de Arana, mistress of Colón. After his first voyage, Colón openly recognized Fernando and agreed to support his mother, Beatriz.

Following Colón's triumphant return from his first voyage, Fernando was appointed as page to Prince don Juan, heir to the thrones of Castile and Aragon. Upon the prince's early death, Fernando entered the service of Queen Isabel.

Under her sponsorship, Fernando was tutored by Italian humanists and scholars imported into Spain by the monarchs. From them he acquired an admiration for books and scholarship. At age thirteen, in 1502, Fernando accompanied his father on his fourth voyage to the New World. Later, when he returned to Spain, Fernando joined his uncle Bartolomé Colón and other friends. Their intent was to defend his father in his legal struggle to reinstate his contractual privileges.

In 1509, when his half-brother, the legitimate Diego, was appointed governor of Hispaniola, Fernando accompanied him. But he soon returned to Spain to pursue his studies and to work on a library that he was developing.

Fernando never married, and he died a wealthy man at his home in Sevilla on Saturday, July 12, 1539. He is buried in the Cathedral of Sevilla. I saw his grave site. It is etched with ships around one side of its marble border. I do hasten to add that Fernando wrote the biography of his father during the last years of his life. The tone of the book appears somewhat polemical and even embittered, perhaps reflecting the frustration through which Colón's family suffered during those years. You see, Fernando was very active in the litigation between the crown and the Colón family. He acted as legal advisor to Diego, and later, his wife. I believe that Fernando assembled the materials for his biography in order to defend his familial position against the crown."

"And what of the other Colombinista?" asked Tlacaellel. "What of this Fray Bartolomé de las Casas?"

"He is perhaps the most interesting of the early Colombinistas," replied Quilaztli. "Let me tell you about him so we can all gain an understanding of the Colombinistas.

He was a Dominican friar and a defender of the Colón family interests, partly, I think, because his father had been a friend of Cristóbal Colón.

Friar Bartolomé familiarized himself with the annotated versions of Colón's books. I think that a very important source of information for him was Colón's *Diario.* He was, after all, the copyist of the only known version of the *Diario.*

Let me explain the suspicious circumstances regarding the said *Diario.* The original diary and a copy of it was made in Barcelona, but they both disappeared sometime after 1554. Now, the only known text is an abstract summary made by Las Casas.

Las Casas had made his abstract and summary from the copy of the *Diario* found in Fernando's library. From this he had copied parts which were of special interest to him, abridged other sections, and omitted other parts which seemed, to him, to be of lesser importance.

Or, should I say, he censored parts which would work against Colón's claim? We will never know for sure. To correct errors or to clarify certain points, Las Casas added his own marginal notes. I think Las Casas altered the spirit of the original *Diario,* or falsified its contents to suit his and the Colón family's views. Whatever the case, there is no doubt that Las Casas did introduce some of his own remarks into the actual text of the *Diario."*

"What do you make of that?" demanded Yoanizi. "How do the Colombinistas defend such trickery?"

"His defenders agree," continued Quilaztli, "that he did introduce new remarks. But, they insist, the remarks did not alter the spirit of the *Diario.* The later Colombinistas say that Las Casas made his remarks in good faith and they were not intended to be attributed to Colón. The errors of transcription, they say, are understandable and even arguable in the sense that such errors are quite normal in such work.

For example, Las Casas, in transcribing the entry of

October 13, 1492, wrote the word *teniendo,* meaning holding, instead of *temiendo,* meaning fearing. His defenders say the error was unintentional. In fact, some Colombinistas go so far as to say that Las Casas did not change words, but that it was Colón himself who must have done so inadvertently! Furthermore, they say that Colón made no effort whatsoever to correct his mistakes.

And they say the same things about certain lines that are missing, and the unclear passages that appear in the only known copy of the *Diario* which, of course, was made by Las Casas, the close friend of the Colón family.

I also hasten to add that in his *Historia de las Indias,* Las Casas wrote, 'These are his very words, although some of them are not in perfect Castilian, since it was not the admiral's mother tongue.' Yet, I did not see any evidence, in all of Colón's writings, of any Italian terms. He wrote everything in Spanish. Almost all of his marginal notes are in Spanish and some in Portuguese.

The charge I make is a very serious one. It appears to me that Las Casas falsified the diary to assist the Colón family in its claim that the admiral was the sole discoverer of the New World and that they are meritorious of all benefits owing to that claim."

"Is there anything further you wish to add regarding Las Casas?" asked Yoanizi.

"Perhaps so," Quilaztli said quickly. "It seems that

even though Las Casas helped the Colón family to establish an argument for their claim, he certainly must have felt something akin to guilt, for later he undertook a campaign to slow down, if not stop, the conquest against our people. In response to his report to the crown, *Brevísima Relación de la Destrucción de las Indias* — A Brief Account of the Destruction of the Indies, in which he tried to affect reform in favor of our people, he was named Protector of the Indians. This report was publicized about 1540.

Interestingly enough, his report worked against Spain, for, when her enemies, especially England, obtained a copy, they condemned the Spanish conquest as brutal and cruel although, had England been in the place of Spain, it would not have been different for us, as evidenced by their colonial practices in North America.

Whatever the case may be, Las Casas, in defending Colón's claim, defended all of the European expansion with all of its trappings of imposed sovereignty over all the peoples in the New World."

"And the claim," commented Copil, "is based on the first words of his contract that began with 'The things supplicated and which Your Highnesses give and declare to Cristóbal Colón in some satisfaction for what he has discovered in the Ocean Sea, and for the voyage which now with the aid of God, he is about to make therein, are as follows, etc.' How do the Colombinistas defend the vagaries of that phrase, especially if the Las Casas copy is in serious question?"

Quilaztli responded, for the questions concerned what he had learned about the history of the past and future. "The Colombinistas," he said, "have tried to show that either Las Casas was copying what he saw, or, admittedly, he was careless in some cases. Take, for example, the phrase you have just quoted. In his *Historia de las Indias,* Las Casas repeats that phrase, but he has changed the tense to read, 'in some satisfaction for what *he will discover* in the Ocean Sea.' It is clear that 'has discovered,' and 'he will discover,' have two different meanings.

It is known that Las Casas had Colón's documents in his hands. Why, then, would he change the meaning of such an important phrase, especially since it would work against the interests of the Colón family?

Could it be that the original contract was also mistranscribed by a scribe? The most curious aspect of the history of the contract is that, despite the fact that it was written in Santa Fe de Granada in 1492, it was not confirmed until four years later in Burgos, although, I suppose, one could argue that the crown ratified it in 1493.

The point of all this is that, from the time of its creation, how many times was it copied and recopied before it was ratified and confirmed years later? And, given the time in between, the crown would have had time to edit the contract of any strange wording before it passed on its confirmation in 1497.

Thus, it appears that Las Casas had a corrected version of the contract, the one that was actually approved. It does cast some limitations on the extent of Colón's claim, that is, what was promised to him in the contract.

While on this subject, I might add that, interestingly enough, the chronicler and cosmographer, Alonso de Santa Cruz, about 1550, wrote *Crónica de los Reyes Católicos.* This work contains, among many rare documents, a copy of the contract. But Santa Cruz, like Las Casas, also edited documents, or he summarized or paraphrased them. His copy of the contract reads, 'that he *ought to discover* in the Ocean Sea.'

Given all of this, the whereabouts of the original contract is also in doubt.

It is known that, between 1520 and 1526 it was conserved in the archive of Santa María de las Cuevas in Spain. But, when I visited the future, that is, five hundred years hence, the original was not to be found.

This is significant because the disappearance of the original copies of those records, which had been approved by the crown, has allowed the Colombinistas to say what they wish. They could do this because now no one could prove otherwise.

The Colombinistas while away their time, concentrating on minutia. This is a device which serves to distract others from the real issue. The real issue is, how legitimate was Colón's claim? They have not addressed our issue, created by Colón, and abetted by the Colombinistas, to wit: a heritage based on a lie."

"Aside from all this vague history of the Colón claim, a history created by missing words, badly transcribed copies, and lost documents, what else have the Colombinistas done to advance the historical claim of Colón?" asked Copil.

"They have written thousands of books." Quilaztli paused for a brief moment. "Each book repeats the same message — that Colón was a genius, a man of vision, a man of courage, a man who did what none other dared to do. To him alone, they have written over and over, belongs the praise for the discovery of a new world.

The Colombinistas created a hero and they have attempted to deify him. Stopping at nothing, they have even pressured to get their highest religious court in Rome to beatify him, and to try to make him a saint. They wanted to make him a saint because his discovery of us began the spread of Christianity to the New World.

They have written songs, poems, plays and histories in order to teach their point of view of him to each succeeding generation."

Chapter 12

Days of Judgement

A sharp sound pierced the ears of Quilaztli. Tilini, Tleume and Caudi stood facing each other as they played music from their flutes. Suddenly, the pitch of the flutes zoomed to an unbelievably high, sharp sound.

The intense pain in Quilaztli's brain caused him to deepen his comatose state. In his unconscious condition he saw flashes of future European conquests: Hernán Cortés and the conquest of the Azteca kingdom; Francisco Pizarro and the brutal war against the Inca Empire; Hernando de Soto's travails in the exploration and attempted conquest of Florida; Francisco Vázquez de Coronado and the war against the Pueblos of New Mexico, and other conquerors like Sir Walter Raleigh, George Oglethorpe, George Washington, Daniel Boone, Andrew

Jackson, Davy Crockett and Kit Carson. *All of them,* thought Quilaztli, *were killers of my people.*

In his mind's eye he caught a glimpse of a vanishing race. Vaguely he could discern white men killing large herds of buffalo, and he could see millions of the dead animals, their carcasses rotting on a great plain, while thousands of Indian men, women and children starved to death on a snowy ground.

He saw the terrifying vision of blond men in blue coats smearing small pox on blankets to give to his people.

Far into the future, he witnessed a shocking scene. It happened at a far away place called Wounded Knee. He could see Anglo American soldiers surrounding a defeated Dakota tribe on a cold snowy day. Captured Indian men, women and children, disarmed and beaten, huddled to keep warm. Suddenly, a cracking noise, like that of a rifle firing, was heard. Surprised by the sound, the soldiers, with powerful weapons, opened fire on the unsuspecting captives. A great number of them, unarmed, were killed or wounded. The year was 1890.

It marked the end of the permissible slaughter of his people.

It marked the passage of almost 400 years since Colón's discovery of the New World.

Quilaztli now knew that the European occupation of the Americas was irreversible; it was not as if his people could beat back the invaders on all fronts. He also knew that the fate of his people, and others like them under the Europeans, would continue for hundreds of years.

Broken treaties, reservations, and forced marches were the business of his peoples' future history. His mind filled with the images he had seen that night.

Eerie images crossed his mind. One was the Trail of Tears. Others were many wars with hollow victories spaced across centuries between the Pueblo Revolt of 1680 and Custer's Last Stand in 1876.

Tears streamed from his eyes as he could foresee the pestilence and despair that awaited his people, even under the best of rulers.

In North and South America, he saw a string of forts with armed Europeans intent on taking Indian lands and lives on the flimsiest of pretexts. There would be no end to the excesses of the European invaders.

Quilaztli saw the rise of Indian leaders and witnessed their defeats. From Pontiac's Rebellion to Geronimo's capture, there was little remedy for the Redman's condition. The colonials, too, readily knew the Redman's lack of defense against European diseases, as well as against drugs and alcoholic concoctions. In the colonial world, poverty would be the Redman's fate.

Perhaps the greatest Indian statesman, the Zapotec Benito Juárez, for whom a city would be named, would state it best: "History will judge your perversity."

When Quilaztli awakened in the forest, he was unable to stand up. Crawling toward a tree trunk, he propped himself against it. Dazed and squinting his eyes in the bright light that flooded the forested shrine, he looked about him.

Everyone — Tlacaellel, Yoanizi, Copil and the other Azteca priests were dead. The ethereal atmosphere of eternity had been replaced by the reality of its earthly counterpart.

Did all this really happen? he asked himself.

Hours later, Quilaztli sat on one of the large rocks that surrounded the burnt Azteca shrine in the forest.

Quilaztli, trembling with fear, buried his face in his hands, and wept.

"What has happened tonight in this forest," Tilini interrupted Quilaztli's sobbing with a soft, soothing voice, "is that you and your brethren have seen the unhealed wound that will fester as a sign of injustices against Indian America.

You asked to see the future.

We showed it to you.

What you saw, with all of its tragedies, was the beginning to end a wrong, like an evil that precedes the good, like the bad deed that precedes the apology."

Quilaztli looked up and said, "But why must it take so long? How long can we endure? How long can my people last against the onslaughts that appear in the colonial records of all the Europeans?"

In fatherly tones, Tilini responded. "You will endure as long as it takes. The historical process is a part of the human condition. It takes time to make an accord. It takes time to make the majority of men of one mind, and only then can the next step be taken.

Mankind marches in uneven ranks, and only when a cadre gains a foothold does an idea begin to take hold.

The mistreatment of your people is a part of the whole. Since the beginning of time, man has mistreated man. That is the human tendency.

Thus it is so that the world must change within the due course of human affairs. Only then will such a tendency be drowned in a sea of goodwill spawned in an enlightened era. It is coming. It is coming!"

"Will it come in my lifetime?" Quilaztli was quick to ask, as if what he had learned was not real. He hoped that what he had learned was only a bad dream.

"Not in your lifetime, nor in your great grandchildren's lifetimes," answered Tilini.

Quilaztli then heard the hollow, haunting voice of Caudi. "It will come after a long struggle," he began. "It will come after colonialism has run its course through the European and American cultures that have embraced it.

New societies will emerge after three world wars have consumed the evils of colonialism. It will come after the last vestiges of colonialism are destroyed in parts of the world far from here in time and space, and where other native peoples struggle for freedom as in the Africa and the Middle East of the future.

Colonial boundaries that have divided the world will change, and those large republics built on imperialism will collapse upon themselves.

Only then will an effort be made to eradicate the inequalities produced over centuries of injustice upon injustice.

In the meantime, your people, and others like them, must continue to endure the struggle. Truth and knowledge are the enemies of ignorance. That is why we have brought you here.

Reflect upon what is before you, so you may let others know that a strain of justice runs through the fabric of the colonial world. Learn. Learn that, even among colonials, there are some who seek justice. Know that the travails of the Colón family parallel the course of colonialism.

What has happened this night in the forest begins a decline of colonialism despite the appearance that it is rising. Before it passes, many horrible things will have transpired. You must record them all for your people, so they may know what faces them. It is truth and knowledge that spawn hope and regeneration."

Then the sad voice of Tleume filled the air. "Be assured, Quilaztli, that colonialism will pass. A great awakening will follow, and native peoples around the world will be set free from the yoke of a colonialism that enslaved them.

As a signal that the change will have commenced, the world will witness a day when the heroes of colonialism will no longer be heroes. Instead, they will be scorned as evil purveyors of the harm they have done to your people.

As a sign, descendants of colonials will point their fingers, accusing one another of the worst crimes against humanity.

As a sign, Colón's descendant will one day visit the New World with repentance in his heart and offer a symbolic gesture, making an attempt to right a wrong that began with his ancestor.

As a sign, before the end of half a millennium, Colón's image will have been splattered with the blood of a sacrificial animal for all the world to see.

The great awakening is yet to come."

With that, Tilini, Tleume and Caudi were gone. The ghostly echoes of their words filled the air and the tree tops of the forest. Quilaztli was left to ponder all that he had learned.

I will commence my history this day, and say all that must be said, beginning with all that has occurred this night. Perhaps my work can, in some small way, be a preparation for the great awakening that is to come.

Overhead, stars twinkled and comets streaked across the night sky. In a short while, dawn would begin a new era. Quilaztli could only shudder at its prospects.

THE ILLUSTRATIONS

Columbus's fleet. From a manuscript of 1583, reproduced in Edward Everett Hale's *The Life of Christopher Columbus.* Chicago: G.L. Howe & Co., 1891.

Bartolomé de Las Casas, 1474-1566, who transcribed Columbus's *Journal.* From F.A. MacNutt, *Bartolomew de Las Casas.* Cleveland: A.H. Clark Co., 1909.

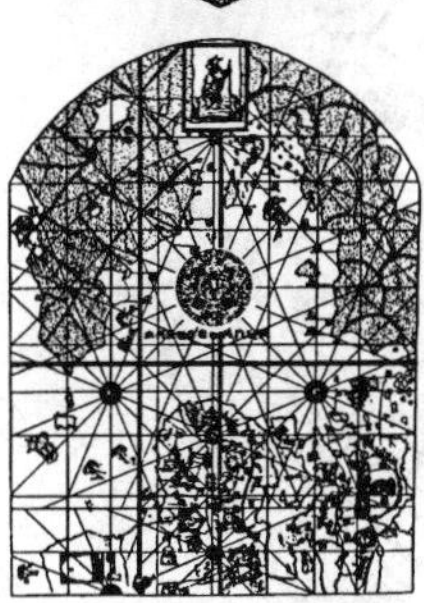

Map drawn in 1500 by Juan de la Cosa, Columbus's pilot. From *Appleton's Annual Cyclopaedia and Register of Important Events of the Year 1892.* New York; Appleton, 1893. Slightly modified.

Note: Illustrations listed above as reproduced in *BIBLIOGRAFIA COLOMBINA 1492-1990: Books, Articles and other Publications on the Life and Times of Christopher Columbus.* Compiled by Joseph P. Sánchez, Jerry L. Gurulé, and William H. Broughton. A Black Knight Publication of The Spanish Colonial Research Center. University of New Mexico, Albuquerque.

Page 132: Illustration adapted from a photograph of a Spanish helmet by Sal Barajas, chair of publication committee of *Letras y Colores,* Centro Cultural de la Raza, San Diego, California.

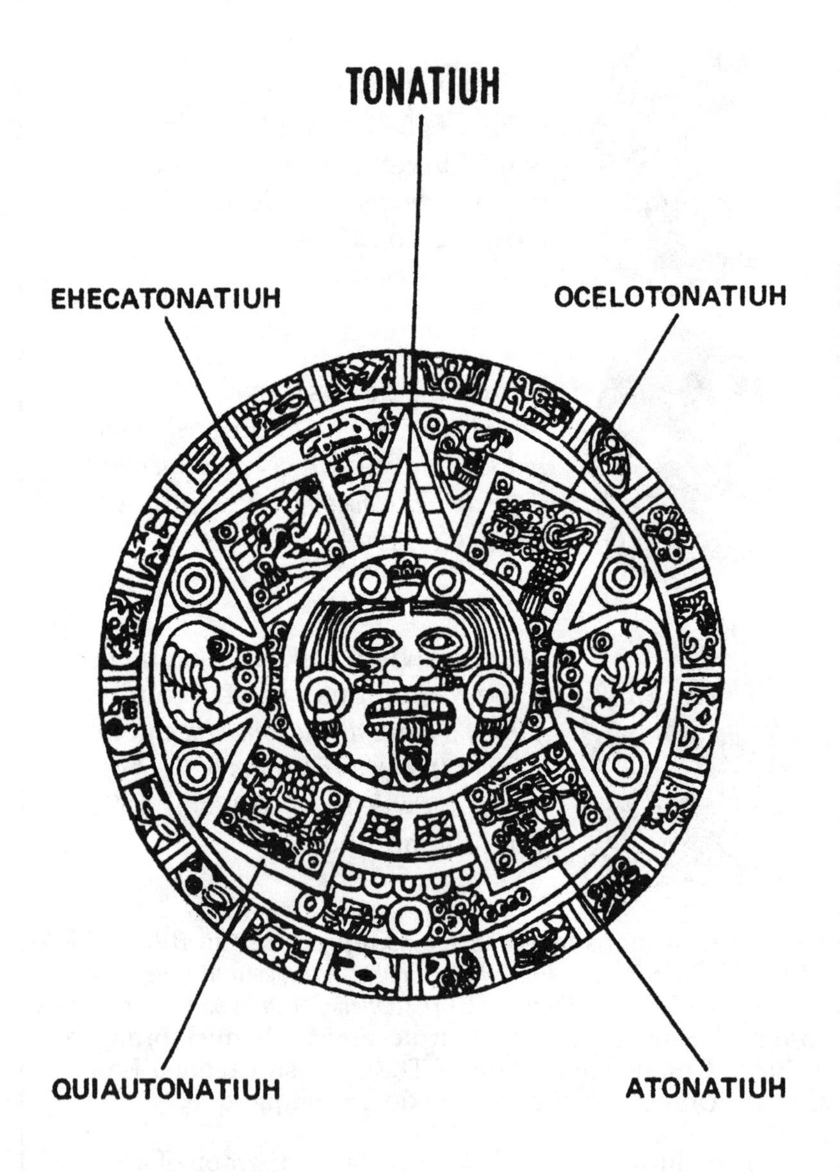
TONATIUH
EHECATONATIUH
OCELOTONATIUH
QUIAUTONATIUH
ATONATIUH

OCELOTONATIUH
(First Sun)

Primer Sol. Sun of Jaguar. First Epoch. Gods create giants who live in caves, eat wild fruits, roots, and do not till the soil. Finally attacked, devoured by jaguars.

EHECATONATIUH
(Second Sun)

Segundo Sol. Sun of Wind. Second Epoch. At end, all is destroyed by strong winds. Gods transform humans into apes to better cling for protection from hurricanes, thus the similarity between humans and simians.

QUIAUTONATIUH
(Third Sun)

Tercer Sol. Sun of Fire Rain. Third Epoch. At end, everything is extinguished by rain of lava and fire. Humans, transformed into birds, are saved.

ATONATIUH
(Fourth Sun)

Cuarto Sol. Sun of Water. Fourth Epoch. At end, great storms, torrential rains, floods, cover the earth to mountain tops. Gods change humans into fish, save them from the deluge.

TONATIUH
(Fifth Sun)

Quinto Sol. The Sun. Fifth Epoch. Time in which we live. The present, during which TONATIUH (Light) struggles daily against the god of night and darkness.

Olmec multi-ton basalt sculpture. La Venta Culture, Veracruz, Mexico. Nearest basalt quarry is 165 miles distant. From Ferdinand Anton, *Ancient Mexican Art,* G.P. Putnam's Sons, New York. 1969

Counter Colón-ialismo Codex, by the Texas Chicana and Chicano artists Sylvia Orozco and Pio Pulido. Based on the Indigenous codices of the 16th century.

The landing of Columbus. Unidentified painting. Probably from the Instituto de Cultura Italiana.
Reproduced in *Excelsior: Ideas, Ediciones Especiales,* #13, Mexico. 1992

From the Códice Mendocino.
The founding of Tenochtitlan at Lake Texcoco by the Mexica. Site of present-day Mexico City.

Cover: TEZCATLIPOCA
The Azteca God of Education. From *THE MEXICAN AMERICAN HERITAGE* The History of Mexican Americans in the U.S., by Carlos M. Jiménez. Third printing. TQS Publications 1995

Book layout, design and graphics:
Octavio I. Romano-V.

Cover by:
Branko E. Romano